"Love On The Verge"

The Ultimate Betrayal

BY B.T.CLARKE

TABLE OF CONTENTS

Chapter 1

"If Perfect Was A Family, We'd Be It."

Hi there! Come on in, welcome. My name is Alexis, aka "Lexi boo" and I would like to invite you into my loving yet chaotic topsy-turvy world. I live in a small town of roughly 500 people, called Monachoy. It's about ten minutes outside the Mississippi stateline, and in this small town everybody knows everybody. No secret is kept and no crime is escaped. I live with my mother Karla Samuels, my father Kenton Samuels, and my little brother KJ Samuels - it's your typical american bi-racial family. People admire our beautiful tri-leveled brown and white brick house with its red door and white-picket fence, and our welcoming mailbox that shouts, "The order of love starts with respect."

Most people claim their family is perfect, but I think if you looked up perfect in the dictionary, you would see mine first. My dad, Kenton Samuels, would come first, of course. A family man, with five brothers and two sisters. A man of Jamaican descent who grew up in New Orleans and was raised by a single mother named Novey. If you saw this light brown-skinned man with curly black hair and freckles around his eyes, you would never guess he worked as a stripper in a local strip club in New Orleans or made Po boy sandwiches at a local dive while putting himself through medical school. This amazing heart surgeon never gets tired of me poking fun at his little black goatee, affectionately named "little pookie bush".

But perfection doesn't stop there. It includes my loving mother, who I claim is the sweetest person in the world. Karla Samuels is only 37 years old and of Caucasian/Asian descent. Her 5'5" frame looks up to my fathers 6'2" stature, and we tease her about It, but her fashion sense more than makes up for this. I tell people Mom is a mashup of Taraji P. Henson and Kim Kardashian with beautiful black body wave type hair, hazel eyes, and a beauty mark above the left side of her lips. You may wonder why an ER nurse would be so concerned with fashion, but mom grew up very spoiled and makes sure KJ and I have everything we need. This West Coast girl (San Diego, CA) is a perfect match for my New Orleans father.

I want to say perfection stops there, but let's not forget my 13 year old brother Kenton, or KJ, as we call him. KJ has mom's height and dad's features, minus the goatee. I call him my thirteen year old "pain" because he lives to play jokes on me and do nothing but play Fortnite every day. I remember mom and dad saying they wouldn't have another child after me, but here he is, so I guess I have to love him. If I have to say something nice, I'll give the boy props because he has my mom's fashion sense - girls definitely notice KJ and we now call him "the Chick magnet". If he plays his cards right, KJ will grow up to be an excellent athlete, since he plays anything from tennis to basketball. He's the quarterback for his school and is a really talented player. Dad swears KJ will be the next All-American.

I'll throw myself into this perfect little family. Me, Alexis Samuels, even though people call me Lexi boo. If you saw me, you would see my mom, although I share dad's curly hair. I think I look like Anissa from my favorite television show "Black Lightning". But I'm a typical girly-girl - dance team at school, loves to shop for anything, and loves hanging out with my bestie Kaylee while singing karaoke on a Friday night. I'm also a typical teenager who turns 16 in one week. Both me and KJ are very excited about the huge party mom has planned for this occasion. Sweet sixteen WOOHOO!

"Who do you want to bring to the party?" asked mom in her normal sweet voice.

"I would like to invite all my friends including Laurence", I replied hastily. Laurence is my new crush in my sophomore class at Cambridge High school - he's cute and tall with beautiful cold black hair and a smile to die for. Kaylee and I obsess - and drool - over him.

"What about KJ?", asks my concerned mother.

"KJ wants to invite his little girlfriend over" I said without too much emotion. KJ wasn't happy for me, he just wants his eighth-grade girlfriend from Cambridge Middle school around.

As you can tell, our family does everything together - perfection. Most families have a "family night", but everyday is Family Day in the Samuels household. I wish all families could be this close - we love everything from sports to game nights to eating dinner together. Dad doesn't even care if we clown him about his stinky feet when he takes his shoes off at the dinner table after a long day at work. He laughs it off and pretends like it doesn't smell like cheddar cheese on a 80 degree summer's day. I often reminisce about how mom and dad met 17 years ago, in the parking lot of the hospital where dad completed his residency. After dad hit mom's car, he left a note on her windshield so she could contact him. It was love at first call.

Again, if "perfect" were a thing, the Samuels family would be that thing. I never saw mom and dad argue (and even when they did, it was never in front of me or KJ). Mom continually reminds us that KJ and I are the best blessings any mom can ask for. Suddenly my quiet moments were interrupted.

"Babe, I'm late, I have to rush out", said dad as he ran for the door. He kissed mom, then me, then gave KJ a high-five while wishing him luck in today's game. But this was typical, all love, no drama.

"Lexi, do you have the guest list for your party?" asked mom.

"Yes, I do. And I will personally invite Laurence", I gushed with a big cheesy smile on my face.

"Wonderful. But do me a favor". I held my breath for one second. "Please invite Laurence to dinner and game night before inviting him to the party". I was relieved. This was an easy task. We both agreed on the following night for dinner. KJ and I kissed mom on the cheek and we heard "have a great day at school" as we rushed out the door.

I forgot how long it took to get to school, but when I arrived, I saw Kaylee standing next to her car, waiting for me. I was the first friend she met when her family moved to Monachoy seven years ago. I knew she was a year older than me, and I was happy and jealous that she already had her license to drive - and her own car! Being from Hawaii, she has beautiful features, and I am very happy to call her my bestie. We did our typical "HEY GIRL!" and laughed. We walked into the building and we stopped in our tracks.

"He's so fine", I remarked as I saw Laurence walking down the hall. He was like a walking movie. His hair flowed with the wind as he gave everyone high-fives. He approached me and Kaylee, and for some reason, that made me nervous and I started to shake.

"He-he-he-lllo, Laurence. Would you, um, like to, um, come for, uh, dinner, uh, tomorrow?"

This was embarrassing. Kaylee noticed drool dribbling from my bottom lip. Nobody ever had this effect on me, nobody!

Kaylee caught the drool as it dropped from my bottom lip. I quickly ran to the restroom. I was embarrassed beyond belief. Kaylee caught up to me and said, "Hey, Laurence is standing outside the door. He's waiting on you". We both stared at each other for a moment. I quickly grabbed a paper towel from the dispenser and wiped my mouth.

"All good?" I asked nervously.

"All good" replied Kaylee.

I headed towards the door and slowly opened it. There he was, my perfect vision. I began talking very fast.

"Whoa, calm down, it's okay" said my perfect vision back to me. He held my hands and then said, "Don't worry, drooling happens to the best of us!"

I could have died right there.

Instead, my perfect vision and I laughed to kill the awkward moment. I looked deep into his perfect brown eyes and finally asked him, "Would you like to join my family for dinner and games tomorrow night?".

"It should be fine, but let me check with my parents first, okay?"

"Sure, no problem", I replied coolly and without drool this time.

My perfect vision started to walk away and as soon as he was gone, I noticed myself jumping up and down with the biggest smile on my face.

" Much better that time," said Kaylee as she joined me a few minutes later. She happened to eavesdrop and heard the whole conversation from the restroom door.

I was elated that Laurence wanted to have dinner with me.

"You know I am super amped right now", I told Kaylee without even looking at her.

"Hey, you don't have to tell me" replied my bestie. "You look like you're bouncing, not walking".

"Let me call my mom before I forget", I replied. I didn't want mom picking me up from school.

The phone rang and rang, but there was no answer.

"She isn't picking up", I told Kaylee. "I think she's busy getting ready for my birthday party".

I didn't want to worry about mom, and there was nothing that could ruin my day after my handsome crush said yes to dinner.

Kaylee dropped me off at home after practice. I waved to her as she drove away and then walked in the house. "HELLO", I yelled loudly. No response. Where was everyone? As I walked into the kitchen to get something to drink, I was stunned by a sudden, disturbing CRASH upstairs. My heart stopped for a moment.

I walked slowly to the door, grabbed my umbrella from the bin, and slowly climbed the stairs, not knowing what to expect at the top. I had a mixed bag of feelings just ten - total horror mixed with total elation from seeing Laurence. Was I ready for what lay in waiting upstairs?

"Get a grip", I told myself.

I finally reached the top stair and then I heard mom and dad yelling at each other. I was in shock - I never heard them yell or argue before. This was so new to me. All I could do was just sit on that top stair and listen.

"I am so tired of you working so late all the time. You rarely have time for your family anymore!" yelled my mom to my dad.

"You know how stressful my job is, I *really* don't need this extra stress from you!" yelled dad in return. "You are such a NAG, I wish I never married you!"

"You bastard!" screamed mom. "Go to hell! Better yet, go find a divorce lawyer if you're that unhappy!"

I couldn't believe my ears. What happened to my picture-perfect parents? What could possibly have triggered this horrible fight between them? These were the two people I looked upon as role models for love, guidance and protection. I was devastated that they arrived at this point. Suddenly, mom ran out of the room, tears streaming down her face. She glanced at me, then disappeared behind the bathroom door.

I couldn't move. I just sat there and blamed myself. "Maybe I put too much pressure on them. Maybe I should get a job so they wouldn't have to take care of me". All sorts of thoughts came rushing into my head. If dad had to work so much, how could I help him take some of the load off his shoulders? I felt the tears start to run down my face, but that's when KJ walked in. I wiped the tears away from my face and ran down to see him.

"Hi KJ, how was your day?"

"Okay, I guess. Anything exciting happen today?"

I was silent.

"Hey, I'll help you with your homework."

A few minutes later, dad walked downstairs and his face did not betray the devastated emotions of just a few minutes ago.

"What's up kids, how was school?" he said nonchalantly.

"School was good", I replied, playing off his dramatic change. "Laurence is coming to dinner and game night tomorrow".

"Alright, sounds good, Lex. Well, I'll see you both in the morning. I'm, uh, working late tonight".

Again. Another late night.

"Okay, dad. Love you. Have a good night at work", as KJ and I both echoed in unison.

Just as my dad left, my face dropped like a heavy sack.

"What's wrong, Lex?", asked KJ.

"Nothing, I'm just tired. I'm going to lay down, okay?"

KJ didn't respond, because he didn't think anything of what I said. I went upstairs to my room and found mom in the bathroom across from my room. The door was ajar and I could hear her sobbing. There was pain in those tears, as though she was being beaten. I didn't know what to do. So I went into the bathroom and started rubbing her back.

"Mom, everything will be okay. Do you believe that?"

"I'm sorry, Lex. I'm sorry I'm crying now, I always want to be strong for you and KJ, but now I look so weak".

I never saw mom as weak before. What do you say to someone who has never been weak before?

"Mommy, you're a very strong woman and an amazing mother. KJ and I are lucky to have you in our lives. Even strong people cry". I didn't believe that, but I was hoping it helped her.

As I hugged her, she thanked me. "Lex, don't worry, I still love your father. Couples fight sometimes".

Yes, but my parents don't. How do I guarantee this never happens again? My mind was racing now. I wanted to end this whole scene, I wanted to put a stop to all this sadness. I kissed mom on the cheek and continued to my room.

I could not sleep that night. This threw me for a loop. What do other kids do when their parents fight? How come I never saw my parents fight before? Does KJ know that they fight? So many questions, but not one answer. Something deeper was going on in this house and eventually the truth would come out.

Morning came quickly, and I woke up with a huge boost of energy. Where was this energy coming from? The horrors of yesterday were pushed to the back of my mind, and guess who made it to the front? Laurence.

I had to look good today for Cambridge High. I had to be the center of attention today. I summoned my fashion sense and picked the cutest outfit in my closet. After running downstairs to have breakfast, I noticed KJ and dad sitting at the table and mom next to the stove, drinking her usual - caramel mocha coffee. It was strange seeing mom and dad today, as if nothing happened the day before.

"Lex, is Laurence joining us for dinner tonight?", asked mom in her usual sweet tone.

"Yes, he is. He texted me last night and confirmed", I said with glee. That made mom smile.

"Ok, I'll run to the store to get something really nice for dinner tonight after dropping you guys off".

"I'm late. Lex, I can't wait to meet the boy", said dad hastily.

"Daddy, his name is Laurence", I sternly corrected him.

"Where are you going?" asked mom as dad was still a blur.

"I forgot that I had a meeting this morning," said the man racing out of the house.

Mom looked upset, because dad had just gotten home from work. I could see the emotions coming in, but a quick glance at KJ and me erased those emotions.

"I'll be home for dinner to meet Laurence", said dad. At least he remembered "the boy's" name!

KJ and I waited a half hour before mom took us to school. I was so pumped that I would see both Kaylee and Laurence today. As we pulled up, I noticed Kaylee first.

"Kaylee, where is Laurence? Have you seen him?" I asked nervously.

"Not yet, maybe he's running a little late", she replied.

Laurence was nowhere to be found. What happened? Then, I received my answer.

"Laurence texted me, he said he will see you tonight. He had a doctor's appointment and couldn't come to school", said Jason, who sat behind me in homeroom class.

Whew! I felt such relief. I was hoping Laurence didn't stand me up. I couldn't wait for school to be over. All I wanted to do was to help mom with dinner for tonight. It had to be perfect.

When the last school bell rang, I grabbed Kaylee by the hand and we ran down the hall and out the door so fast. We jumped into the car and I told her to drive as fast as she could, that there was no time to waste! After we reached home, I promised her I would give all the beautiful details of tonight's festivities.

I walked into the house and found mom cooking and singing with the music on blast. The music was contagious and I found myself singing and dancing while setting the table. I wondered why mom was so happy.

"Mom, are you feeling better since yesterday?"

"Never better, Sweetpea. Your dad and I made up over the phone today, and I'm feeling great! He's also taking off a few days to spend more time at home with us". That was music to my ears.

I was happy because I love spending quality time with my family. Was everything getting back on track? I thought to myself. Then KJ walked in.

"KJ, please go shower and get ready for dinner", said mom in her upbeat voice.

"Lex, did you give Laurence the address and the time?" said mom, now directed to me.

"Yes, I gave it to his friend, Jason, in class today."

With that, I went upstairs to get ready for dinner. I had 2 hours to get cute. After all this was my big night. I climbed those stairs like someone was chasing me.

I wanted to look good for Laurence, but what would qualify as "good" tonight? After searching my wardrobe for about an hour, The winner was my pink cashmere sweater, blue jean mini skirt, and my pink Gucci sandals. After a good shower and leg shave, I got dressed. I fluffed my curls, put my glossy pink lip gloss on and took a final full body view in the mirror. I looked good! After a few seconds of self-admiration, the doorbell rang.

Laurence. The time has come. I was beside myself. My heart was beating so fast. I had to calm myself down. When I reached the stairs, I started walking down slowly. Poetry in motion, and then it happened.

My left leg went right up from under me as I tumbled down the last four stairs. What just happened? Did anyone notice that? Unfortunately, yes. Dad and Laurence ran to help, and dear old KJ just couldn't stop laughing. This had to be the worst day of my life. I knew I shouldn't have tried so hard to look so good.

"I'm so sorry, Laurence, I'm a real clutz sometimes", I said sheepishly.

"Don't worry about it, I love the way you bounced back up after hitting the bottom of the stairs, are you okay?", asked my perfect vision.

"Yes, I'm fine", I lied. My leg was hurting so bad, but I played it cool. We all sat down and ended the stair debacle.

Suddenly mom and dad were playing tug-of-war with Laurence. Mom wanted him by me, but dad wanted him closer to his side of the table. Knowing dad, he wanted to keep an eye on my boo. We just wanted dad to be on his best behavior.

Mom prepared my favorite meal - Lasagna with four meats, garlicky garlic bread, and spinach salad with zesty Italian dressing. What could be better than this? My favorite foods, my family getting along, and my future boyfriend - all under the same roof at the same time.

"Laurence, what are your plans with my daughter?", asked dad.

I couldn't believe it. Dinner just started and dad asked this question?

"Dad, please don't embarrass me", I retorted.

"Sweetheart, I'm not trying to embarrass you, I just want to know what this young man's intentions are with my baby girl".

"Sir", said Laurence slowly, "Lexi and I are just friends right now. She seems really cool, and I want to get to know her better."

Those last words hung in the air like smoke from a thousand cigarettes. The next reply shook the house.

"BETTER? WHAT DO YOU MEAN BETTER?" screamed dad, with a face to match.

"Dad, calm down, you're getting really upset", I intervened. "Can I see you in the kitchen?"

Once in the kitchen, I laid it on the line with him.

"Dad, why are you embarrassing me like this? I really like this guy, I'm trying to impress him." I pleaded.

"Lexi, there's no need to impress a boy that you will never date."

I was furious with this response and demanded an explanation.

"Lex, you're my little girl. Our job is to protect you".

I held back my anger. "PROTECT ME FROM WHAT!?" was all I could say.

"Protect you from little boys with hidden agendas" was his closing argument.

I had no words left in me. All I could do was stomp back to the dinner table, angry.

"Is everything okay?" asked mom, genuinely concerned.

"Ask the man you married", I shot back. I was so upset with dad since he was being unreasonable with everyone. I was confused - dad seemed happy to meet Laurence but seconds later he's being grossly unfair. What happened?

Mom seemed to ignore this and just asked if we had enough to eat and were ready for game night to begin. Dad ran into the living room like a two-year old boy. He acted like I wasn't mad at him - but I was. He picked our first game for the night - Taboo.

"Nice choice Dad," said KJ.

Still steaming from dad's behavior, I looked over at Laurence and he smiled at me. All of the madness went away. I teamed up with Laurence and we played against mom and dad. We asked KJ to be our scorekeeper. Laurence and I were perfect together.We scored four out of five in the first round and mom and dad only got two correct.

"We beat your butts," said Laurence at the top of his lungs. He was hyped! Dad didn't appreciate this because Taboo was his game and he always won. But tonight was different.

Tonight would see a new champion.

Tonight made dad a loser. And this made him even more competitive.

First came the push-up contest. Then came the jumping-jack contest. And finally, the bake-off contest.

"Daddy, really?" I asked unamused. This competition was becoming too much for me and mom. KJ, on the other hand, was devouring every moment of this fiasco. I suddenly noticed the time.

"Daddy, Laurence has to call his mom to pick him up, it is getting kind of late."

"Okay", replied my sweaty father. "Laurence, it was good meeting you, man. We have to do this again."

"Absolutely, sir" replied this perfect guy. "I had a GREAT time with all of you tonight, thanks for having me over".

"You are welcome anytime", said mom with a smile.

I took Laurence out on the deck and he called his mom to pick him up. We chatted while we waited. It dawned on me how funny Laurence really was. I didn't really know him well enough, but we had so much in common. We both like R&B music, karaoke, and hanging out with our families.

"I really enjoyed hanging out with your family tonight. Your dad is pretty cool", he remarked.

I didn't know what to say. Dad was pretty mean tonight, after all. I stayed silent, and then I heard...

"When I first saw you in homeroom class, I thought you were the most beautiful girl I had ever seen."

My heart froze for a whole minute. How do I respond to that?

I blushed. My smile could be seen a thousand miles away, and it went from ear to ear.

I knew we would hit it off from the moment he walked into school. I felt my cell phone being snatched from my hand.

"Hey -"

Laurence was busy snapping a selfie of himself while adding it to his already saved contact in my phone.

"That pic is something nice for you to look at when you're thinking of me," he giggled.

I was in awe. I could not find the words to express how I felt, but I was in awe.

We saw Laurence's mom pull up, and I walked him to the car. After one big hug, he got in. I was consumed with his smell and hoped it would stay on forever. It smelled like sunshine on a rainy day. I was on cloud nine. When I walked back in the house, my perfect family was sitting on the couch. Every face was lit up with a smile.

"Did you kiss him?" wondered my little nosy brother.

"No, I didn't, little boy", I answered in a very disgusted voice.

"KJ, leave your sister alone", said mom in her motherly tone. "We'll discuss the deets later, girlfriend", she remarked to me in passing. I laughed. Mom was trying so hard to be cool.

"I still don't like him", said my dad.

"Dad, I'm still mad about how you treated Laurence", I shot back.

"I'm sorry, I'm just being a father", he tried to say sincerely. It didn't work. He kissed me on the forehead then headed upstairs.

I sat on the couch and just pondered the evening. I did want the family to like him, but what mattered was how I felt. He made me smile. I was so happy I met him in time for my birthday. All I really wanted was one special dance with a special guy that I liked, on my 16th birthday.

"KJ, what did you think of Laurence tonight?", I asked my brother hesitantly.

"He's cool", said my pithy little pain-in-the-neck. That was good enough for me. KJ left for bed after his honest assessment, and I stared at my phone. A new text message popped up from Laurence:

I enjoyed being with you tonight. You smell like flowers on an April day.

He sure knows how to make a girl smile. What a sweet guy. We texted almost the whole night. Everytime my phone dinged, I felt butterflies in my stomach. I couldn't wait to see him back at school.

Tomorrow is going to be lit, I told myself as I fell asleep.

Chapter 2

"My Mom and Dad"

After having Laurence over last night, I was floating on air, and nothing or no one could kill my vibe. I decided to have lunch with him at school, we laughed the whole time. We even found time to play a small prank on Kaylee, and she loved it.

After Kaylee dropped me off at home, I took a rest stop in the middle of the living room. Adele was playing on the radio, and I danced across the floor as if I was on stage with strobe lights all over me. I was lost in my own world, when all of a sudden -

SLAM!

The sound of the front door being slammed shook the neighborhood. Even Adele's beautiful voice was drowned out. It scared the pee out of me. I stopped in my tracks and slowly turned around.

"Dad? Is everything okay?" He didn't seem okay according to the angry look in his eyes.

"It's nothing, Lex. I'm just tired from work."

"I thought you were taking a few days off from work", I asked, concerned.

"Yes, soon. I don't know when", he responded bleakly. Something seemed off.

"Are you and mom...okay? I asked, again concerned.

"We're fine", he said. He also told me to "stay out of it", whatever that meant.

"I'm confused, dad. What am I staying out of?". I was afraid to hear any answer at this point.

"Lexi", he began, "I'm *not* going to say this again, please stay OUT of it".

That was his final answer. I was not going to push further, so I ran upstairs to shower.

My mind was racing - what is happening between mom and dad? Where are my perfect parents that I enjoyed all these years? As I lay on my bed, all I could think about was the D word. I felt divorce was imminent and I had to prepare for this. But who or what was causing this? Was it something me or KJ did?

My phone interrupted my constant worry. I looked down and saw "Mom" across my screen.

"Hi, mom".

"Hey Lex", replied Mom. "I'm sorry but I have to work a little late tonight. I need you to make dinner for you and KJ."

"Um, what about dad?", I asked, finding it hard to believe that dad would be left out of this conversation.

"That man could rot in hell", mumbled my loving mother under her breath. I had to ask her again.

"Mom, could you repeat that? I don't think I heard you." I hated lying to her.

"Oh, dad can fend for himself", replied mom, in a tone slightly better than before. "I just want to make sure you and KJ are okay." I appreciated the concern, but was worried about dad. I decided not to probe further.

"Ok, mom. I got it". I then heard the obligatory "I love you" and the phone went silent.

After this nerve-wracking call, I sat on the side of my bed wondering what was really going on. I had never seen my parents behave like this towards each other. It was beginning to really bother me, so I called Kaylee.

"Hey, Kay, do you want to come over for dinner? I really need a friend". I was slowly becoming an emotional wreck. As always Kaylee agreed to be there for me. She said yes to coming over.

I went downstairs to prepare dinner. I really felt bad about what my mom said about my dad, even though she mumbled this under her breath. But those words were as loud and clear as any words she had ever spoken to me. I decided to make a little extra food for dad. KJ walked in and I told him that mom will be working late tonight and I was making dinner for us.

"You make dinner?" he laughed.

"Be quiet, KJ", I snapped back. He ran upstairs to get ready to eat.

I heard Kaylee knock on the door. When she entered the house, I noticed a pillow and a big bag.

"What's in the big bag?", I asked.

"Well, by the sound of your voice on the phone, I thought it would be better if I slept over tonight", said my best friend who understood me. "And my parents said it would be okay."

I loved Kaylee for her intuition. I couldn't thank her enough, because I truly needed someone tonight. Who better than my best friend?

During dinner, KJ harassed Kaylee the whole time, I had to send him to his room. After washing dishes, we headed upstairs to my room.

"Lex, is everything okay?", asked Kaylee.

I told her everything that was going on between my parents.

"Wow", she replied. "The same thing happened to my mom and dad before they got a divorce".

Lovely. So this is what I have to look forward to. I took a deep breath and I just felt exhausted. I'm almost 16 years old and now and I have to deal with -- divorce? I didn't know what to do.

"I just want my family to be happy again, because that's what makes me happy", I told Kaylee.

"I know how you feel", she said to me. "I remember how I used to feel during the divorce, and I remember how my parents treated me during the separation."

In other words, get ready for misery. But I knew this wasn't just about me, I had to consider my parents feelings also. I just wanted peace, more than anything else in this world.

"Hey, Lex, I think you'll feel much better if we go for a ride. Ok?" Kaylee was being very helpful.

"Well", I thought out loud, "it's only 7 PM. I think it's a good idea and it may ease my mind a bit. Let me grab my sweater."

"KJ, we're going for a ride and I can't leave you here by yourself, let's go!", " I don't want to go, I'm playing my game. Just leave already" Said KJ. I didn't want to argue, so Kayle and I headed for Cold Stone Creamery for a double scoop. Ice cream always made me feel better. I then called Laurence to see if he was available. He said he was. As we approached his house, I texted him to let him know we were outside. When Laurence got into the car, Kaylee did something I wish she didn't do.

She told Laurence about my parents.

I love Kaylee, but sometimes I wish she held back. I didn't want Laurence to know about my parents fighting. I wanted him to think that my family was loving and close - even "normal". What I started to witness between them was nowhere near "normal".

"There's nothing to be ashamed of, Lexi", he said. "Everyone's parents argue from time to time." He tried to be reassuring, but it didn't help. Kaylee then continued her unbounded honesty by describing her parents divorce. I just wanted all this talk about "divorce" to stop. Forever.

"Lex, how about we go for a walk?" Laurence asked me.

"Sure", I told him. How could I not say yes to him?

We walked down a long gravel path. It had the prettiest pink flower bush that smelled so sweet. Laurence picked up some flowers and handed them to me.

"Lex, what happened with Kaylee's parents will not happen to your parents. What I saw at dinner the other night was pure love. Parents argue sometimes. It's just natural."

After this talk, I became very humbled. Laurence somehow knew how to make me feel better. I felt that everything was going to be okay after spending time with him. We walked back to the car, and Laurence gave me the most comforting hug I had ever gotten. I kissed him on the cheek and got back in the car.

"What did you guys talk about?" asked Kaylee on the way home.

"We just walked and talked. He made me feel better."

"I love how he comforts you. He is definitely a *keeper*", she said emphatically.

She was right. I was really appreciative of that moment with Laurence. On the way home Kaylee blasted some Chris Brown. We danced all the way back to the house. As we pulled up, I noticed KJ sitting on the porch.

"KJ, why are you outside? Why are you crying?". I was so scared that something bad happened because I had left him home alone.

"Mom and dad are fighting, and mom threw the blue glass Vase at dad - the one that grandma gave to us. She missed, but now dad is mad. He pushed her on the sofa."

Suddenly, all my happy thoughts left my body. This seemed like the end to me. I ran into the house. Mom and dad were struggling on the sofa.

"Dad, what are you doing?" I yelled. I tried pulling dad away but he turned around and shoved me to the ground. Finally, mom got one hand free and smacked dad hard in the face. Dad balled his fist and punched mom in the face. Her head fell back on the couch. I pinched myself because this couldn't be real. But sadly it was. Suddenly, there was a pause.

Dad stopped. His eyes widened as he breathed hard. He grabbed his keys and ran out the house.

"Dad, come back" I yelled. I ran after him, but it was too late. The car sped away. I sat on the stairs and just froze. This was the first time in my life that I felt true shock. All I wanted to do was hug and comfort KJ. Kaylee got to KJ first and told him everything was going to be okay.

But everything was *not* going to be okay. I needed to know the truth now.

"Lex, I'm going to go check on your mom", said Kaylee.

I reached for my phone and tried calling dad. It went to voicemail, three times in a row. I almost gave up. My family was falling apart, and there was nothing I could do.

After making sure KJ was safe inside, I walked over to mom. She was sitting on the sofa crying, her head completely down. With Kaylee wiping the blood from her face.

"Mom, are you okay?" I asked.

She looked up at me and started to cry more. I had to comfort her, so I sat beside her and held her as tight as I could. Kaylee and I just sat there with mom until she stopped crying.

I didn't understand how everything got to the point.

"Mom, please tell me what happened," I asked. My mom just looked at me and then said, " Lexi, no matter what happens with me and your dad, please know that we love both you and KJ so much."

I knew this already, but I just wanted to know what happened tonight. I asked again, slowly but with more emphasis, "What happened tonight, mom?" My mom looked into my eyes and said, "Your dad and I just got into a huge disagreement about work, and about him not taking off, and it just escalated from there."

I wondered how it could get to the point of a physical altercation. But I didn't ask. All I knew was that my mom was hiding something, and I needed to get to the bottom of it since no one wanted to tell me what was really going on.

"Mom, are you ready to go to bed?" I asked.

"Yes", she replied. "But let me clean up here, and you and Kaylee go upstairs and get ready for bed. You don't have to help.".

That was a cue to us that she needed to be alone for a few minutes. I saw the sadness in her face, and it broke my 15 year old heart. When we got upstairs, Kaylee and I just stared at the ceiling until we fell asleep.

I couldn't sleep and woke up at 3 AM. Even Kaylee was awake.

"Why are you awake?" I asked her.

"I'm just texting my boyfriend, Jeremy", she whispered.

I walked into my parents bedroom. Dad was nowhere to be found. This is the worst case, I told myself. Mom was on her side of the bed. I went downstairs to avoid waking up mom. There on the table was dad's medical bag. I don't know why, but my intuition told me something was inside that bag. I opened it and shuffled through some papers and samples, Nothing.

Then the briefcase fell off the table onto the floor. *Dang*, I hope that didn't wake up anybody, I thought. I bent down to pick it up and then I noticed the compartment.

The bag had a secret compartment. This was straight out of the movies.

I looked in the compartment and noticed a cell phone. Was this dad's work phone?

I turned it on. The first thing that hit my eyes was an image of some lady - it looked like Mrs. Karen Ellis, the wife of my dad's partner.

Does this mean that dad is cheating on mom? I wondered. I had to stop jumping to conclusions. "Get a grip on yourself" I told my beating heart. I continued searching the phone and then noticed some text messages between my dad and Mrs. Ellis. I was lucky because there was no password on this phone. But what should I do with all these messages? Would these messages lead to the downfall of this family? I decided to take screenshots of everything and send them to my phone. Being cautious, I also deleted the sent history and the screenshots to erase my tracks.

I ran back upstairs to my bed and I wondered if mom knew about all of this? After a few minutes, I cried myself back to sleep.

Chapter 3

"Everyone's Talking"

After the past couple of days, I felt really drained, and my mind was all over the place. I needed to clear my head, so I went out for a walk. It didn't matter where I went, I just needed to go somewhere until everything made sense to me.

I first walked past our neighbor, Ms. Jackson. I waved to her as she was sitting on her porch swing, and she started to utter something back. All I could see was her lips moving. I took off my headphones to hear what she was saying.

"How are you doing?"she asked me.

"I'm doing fine", I lied.

"I heard a bunch of yelling and screaming coming from your house last night," she commented. "Is everything okay?"

I was in no mood to answer this. Ms. Jackson reminded me of Willona Woods from the TV show *Good Times*. The neighbor who loves to meddle in everyone's business.

"Yes ma'am. Everything is fine," I continued to lie. I decided to just move along after that. I kept picturing mom and dad physically hitting each other. I never expected that to happen in a million years. Then my mind shifted to the medical bag and the secret compartment - and that cell phone. How should I tell mom? When should I tell mom? Should I tell my mom?

I walked into the grocery store for some gummy bears.

"Hi Lexi, how's your parents?" asked the owner, Mr. Chancy.

"Fine, they're fine". I was getting comfortable with lying now.

Then the gossip started.

"Did you hear that Kenton Samuels is cheating on Karla with his partner's wife?" said Mrs. Johnson to Mr. Chancy, as I searched for my gummy bears. Mrs. Johnson continued her juicy gossip. "I heard this from my sister, Cheryl, who heard it from Karen Ellis herself".

My mind was blown. I just froze where I was standing. I pretended as if I didn't hear anything. I diverted my attention back to the candy aisle, laser-focused on finding those gummy bears.

But gummy bears were not on my mind. My ears waited for more news from the lips of Mrs. Johnson. The news was coming faster and faster now. Mrs. Johnson continued.

"Karen Ellis caught Kenton Samuels and Dr. Ellis kissing in their office exam room a few nights ago". Suddenly, the text messages and pictures I saw on my dad's phone last night made sense. I became so angry I threw my candy on the floor and ran home to speak to mom. As I reached the front door, I was out of breath. I could not enter the house like this. I gave myself a few minutes to calm down and catch my breath.

"Mom, are you here?" I yelled after walking into the house. I saw her car in the driveway so she had to be home. I ran up the stairs and found mom on the phone, but she didn't hear me.

"Yes, Mr. Chancy, I am fine", I heard her tell the store owner. "No, you really don't have to come over, I am fine. Have a good day" She hung up the phone.

"Mom, we need to talk", I said, as I entered her room.

"Are you okay, Lex? You're breathing sounds a little strained to me", she asked me.

"I'm okay, mom. We need to talk about something that just happened while I was out."

I recounted all the events of the past hour and what I heard Mrs. Johnson tell Mr. Chancy about dad and Dr. Ellis.

"What exactly did you hear, Lex?" she asked.

"I heard that dad and Dr. Ellis are *boyfriends*, and not just *friends*."

Mom laughed at this statement.

"Lex, people here love to gossip. Nothing like that is going on between dad and Dr. Ellis." She sounded so convincing. For a woman who just heard her husband was *kissing another man*, she seemed very calm. I was confused and didn't know what to think. Either she is in denial, or she really doesn't know.

"Does dad have a second phone?" I inquired.

"Yes, of course. He uses that when he's on call", she replied.

"Mom, I went downstairs last night while you were sleeping and I looked inside dad's medical bag."

This upset her immediately. "Alexis, you know better than to poke around in your dad's stuff. He has confidential things in there."

"But, mom", I started, " I didn't go in there for that. I know you and dad are hiding stuff, so I wanted to find out what was going on." Mom assured me she wasn't hiding anything and that both her and dad were just going through a "rough patch".

Famous last words. I couldn't stand there and take this.

"STOP treating me like a little kid!" I screamed, "I AM turning 16 in a few days. I know there's more to all of this, and I WILL find out on my own!"

I walked out of that room and slammed the door behind me. I was both angry and frustrated at the same time. I called for a Lyft to take me to dad's office, since he wasn't picking up any of my calls.

"Lexi, where are you going?" asked mom, as the Lyft pulled up.

"Since you're not being truthful, I'm going to ask dad."

Mom stared at me as the Lyft pulled away. I could see pure hurt all over her face.

While in the car, I kept rehearsing in my head what I wanted to say to my dad, and how I was going to say it. After we arrived, I walked into dad's office and said a polite "hello" to Ms. Brandy, my dad's receptionist. Ms. Brandy was always happy to see me.

"Is my dad available?", I asked.

"Yes, he just got out of surgery. He'll be here in a few minutes."

I sat down and waited patiently, while still rehearsing what I was going to say. Then it hit me.

"Ms. Brandy, have you seen my dad and Dr. Ellis acting...strange lately?" Those were not the words I had rehearsed in my mind. I had to quickly revise that.

"Has my dad been working late, lately?". That sounded better.

"Well," she started, "I only worked late one night a few days ago. Other than that, I've been going home around my usual time. Why do you ask?" I piqued her interest somehow.

"Um, I miss my dad. I'm just wondering when he will take some time off." I hoped that sounded convincing enough.

Ms. Brandy nodded her head, while being completely taken aback by the words coming out of my mouth.

"Hey, Lex", greeted my dad, finally. He gave me a hug, but now was not the time for hugs. "What are you doing here, baby girl?"

"We need to talk", I said, "in your office."

We left Ms. Brandy and sat down in his office.

"Lex, I know why you're here", he started. "What happened between your mom and me was a huge mess. I'm so sorry you and KJ have witnessed our recent spats..."

"Dad", I interjected as my anger started to rise, "how could you put your hands on mom like that? How could you push KJ the way you did?

My voice was getting louder as I continued.

"Lex, please watch your tone. You don't speak to me like that". His voice was firm now.

"I don't care who hears me", I said right back. I was mad and he needed to see this.

This, for some reason, made him calm down.

"I'm sorry, Lex...", he said.

I interrupted him. "Sorry is not why I'm here. I want to know if you're cheating on mom...with a *man*!" The words finally came out. There was no turning back now.

"What?" was the only word he could muster. "What are you talking about...what *man*?"

"Dr. Ellis", I muttered, "Dr. Ellis".

The room got quiet.

"Lex, who told you that? Who has been saying those things to you?". His voice was still calm.

"Everybody, everybody in town is talking about it, and apparently me, KJ, and mom are the only people who don't know about this."

"Lex, it's not what you think", he said, "I would never do anything to hurt my family. I love you guys with every fiber of my being. There is nothing or no one more important to me than you, KJ, and your mother."

I didn't know if I should believe him. His words were so sincere, but what about the text messages I saw on his second phone? I pulled out my phone and looked for the screenshots I captured. I placed the phone where he could see it and said, "Then what about these images? Please explain *that* to me." I would make a great interrogator or detective.

Dad picked up the phone and started reading the messages. I saw his mouth open wide, as if he just saw a ghost.

"That's what I thought!" I said, as I snatched the phone from his hands. I couldn't take any more of his lies.

I sat on the front porch of his office with my head down, and cried into my knees. I don't even remember how long I was there. I called Kaylee to pick me up since she lived only five minutes from here. All I could think about was how my family was being torn apart and there wasn't anything I could do about it. I felt hopeless. But thank goodness for Kaylee - she was the only constant in my life. She always had my back.

After I got home, I went straight to my room. I ignored KJ who was pestering me about my whereabouts. I was so drained from the day. I put on some headphones and blasted music into my head as I fell asleep.

School was no better the next day. I couldn't tolerate anyone, even Laurence. At one point in the day, my friend Cassandra dared to tell me that she heard rumors about dad.

"Hey, I heard your dad is *gay*", she said menacingly.

"Mind your own business", I said Soprano-style.

"Hey, don't be mad at me just because your dad likes to kiss other dudes in the dark."

I was livid. "Cassandra, if you say one more thing about my dad, I will make your whole existence a living hell."

"I'm *sorry*", said Cassandra in a sarcastic tone. I was so ready to end this day. That's when I felt Kaylee grab my hand.

"Lexi, everything is going to be okay", she said to me, "don't worry about Cassandra."

And then I heard it.

"Oh, you're just like your dad. You like girls just like he likes boys."

That was all I needed. The bell rang, and we all ran into the hallway. I grabbed Cassandra's hair and slammed her head into the locker. She had been warned. Cassandra fought back like a wounded animal, but I kept punching her in the mouth. All I could picture was my parents fighting, and all I could feel was my fist on her mouth. I kept hitting until I felt her blood dripping on my hands. That's when the fight ended.

People were staring, but I didn't care. I grabbed by bag and ran home.

What was I turning into? After reaching my room, I looked in the mirror and all I saw was an angry monster staring right back at me. I was becoming a very bad person because of what my parents were going through. I just started crying and screaming at the thought of me turning into this nightmare.

Knock, knock. Who could that be, I wondered?

Kaylee entered the room and gave me a hug.

"Hey, is Cassandra okay?" I asked her.

"Well, it appears she is going to be fine", said Kaylee who tried to reassure me.

I was temporarily relieved, because I feared I had done some serious damage to Cassandra.

"Kaylee, I am so angry right now."

"Lex, don't let anger consume you like this". Kaylee's words were not helping me.

Now we heard another knock downstairs. Who could it be this time?

"Lex, can you come down please?" said mom. This wasn't good, I knew I was in trouble. As I walked downstairs, I noticed two police officers. I saw my life flash before my eyes at that moment.

"Why didn't you tell me you got into a fight at school?" asked mom.

I just shrugged my shoulders, not knowing what to say.

"The young lady you beat up at school now has two broken ribs, a fractured jawbone, and a few teeth knocked out", said one officer without any emotion. "How did this fight start?"

"Officer, Cassandra was being a bully. I asked her to stop but she didn't. Before I knew it, I just snapped."

The truth will set you free, right? Maybe not this time.

Now it was the second officer's turn to speak.

"Does your daughter have anger issues?" he asked my mom.

"No, Lexi is a very good daughter. If she got in any trouble at school, she must have been provoked in some way.".

Good job, mom. That's how a mama bear protects her cubs.

"Well", continued the first officer, "Cassandra and her family want to press charges, but before proceeding, they wanted a statement from your daughter". My mom was shaking now.

The officers continued to describe the gory details of our confrontation, then thanked mom for her time and told her they would be in touch.

Mom stared at me, then walked away.

I felt nothing but shame right then. I was ashamed of my behavior and of all the stress I was placing on mom. I was praying silently that I wouldn't end up in jail and that Cassandra would be okay. This was not how I pictured my Sweet 16 Birthday would end up.

Chapter 4

"HELL HATH NO FURY LIKE A WOMAN SCORNED"

At this point I accepted the fact that all our lives were in shambles now. But I was not prepared for what was about to happen next. It only got worse from here.

I was suspended for two weeks after beating up Cassandra. My mom knew that the drama between her and dad was messing with my sanity. Then one morning mom said to dad, "I've been getting calls from people in town saying that you are cheating on me with Dr. Ellis. Please tell me this is not true."

You could hear pins drop after this statement was made. I didn't hear one word from my dad's mouth. Then mom repeated, "Kenton, you promised me that *that phase* of your life was over. Now you're sleeping around with him? What is WRONG with you? What about our kids? What about ME?"

The anger was rising, along with the tension in the room.

"It's not what you're thinking", said dad. But nothing could stop the tears from mom's face, and nothing could stop her from yelling louder at dad. And then, the truth rolled out.

"ALRIGHT, Karla, you want the *truth*?", shouted dad. "I've been working late nights because Dr. Ellis is buying my part of the Practice so I can spend more time at home with you and the kids. This was going to be a *surprise*, but now you've ruined It!"

Silence.

I wanted to yell "He's LYING", but I held my tongue. I just needed to be a child right now and hold my peace. All this was just too much for me.

Mom just stared at dad, not knowing what to say. The truth was finally hanging over our heads and we had no genuine way to respond to it. Soon after that moment, we all walked around the house like zombies, not saying anything to anybody. I felt bad for KJ. He looked so confused and really had no idea what was going on. I didn't have the heart to tell him anything just then.

As we sat down to eat, there was another knock at the door. I was starting to hate knocking. Every time someone knocked on a door, something bad happened.

The door opened, and there stood a very pregnant lady. I never saw this lady before. We knew everybody in town, and yet, we didn't know who this lady was.

"Can I help you?" asked my curious mom.

"I'm looking for Kenton", said the very pregnant lady.

"I'm sorry, are you one of his patients?". Mom was now in interrogation mode.

"No, but my husband is Kenton's patient," said the unknown lady.

With that, she was let inside.

"Can I get you something to eat or drink?" asked mom, who always tended to people in need.

"No thank you, I'm fine" replied our new pregnant guest.

"Kenton, you have a guest. Can you come here, please?" Mom called out in her accommodating voice.

Dad entered the room and suddenly stopped in his tracks.

"What are you doing here?" said a shocked dad to our pregnant guest.
"I need to speak to you," said the lady in response, calmly.

"OK, what is going on here?" Mom interjected with anger rising steadily.

"Well, Kenton, should *I* tell her, or do *you* want to do the honors?"
My nightmare just took a turn for the worse.

"Tell me WHAT?" screamed mom. Dad just stood there, saying nothing.

"KENTON, WHAT IS GOING ON? TELL ME NOW!" This was the
loudest I've ever heard mom speak to dad.

"Karla", said dad slowly, "this is Jennifer".

"Okay, and just who is *Jennifer*?" screamed mom.

Then came the most horrifying words I have ever heard in my life.

"I am his fiance and the mother of his unborn child. That's who I am"
said our newly revealed pregnant guest, in disgust.

Time froze. We all looked at each other and then back at Jennifer. Did
she say what we thought she just said? My mouth opened so wide I thought
my jawbone would snap. Mom jumped up so fast and approached dad
with Category 5 anger in her eyes.

"WHAT?? Kenton, you mean to tell me you are *actually* cheating on
me with this WOMAN? And you got this thing PREGNANT? And I *know*
she didn't also say she was your FIANCE? How can she be your FIANCE
if you're married??"

I didn't know whether to hit Jennifer or hit dad first. I could not
accept that this pregnant woman is claiming to be dad's fiance, when he
already has a wife!

"Karla, I'm sorry..." begged dad. He was talking so fast it all sounded
like gibberish. Then I noticed mom - she grabbed Jennifer by her shirt and
dragged her out the front door. My mom, who moments earlier was offer-
ing hospitality to a pregnant lady, was now dragging her like a rag doll out
the front door.

After this display of brute force, she calmly turned to KJ and said
"It's time to catch the bus for school". How can someone change in an
instant like that? Who could think of school at a time like this? Mom went

from 100 to 0 in a matter of seconds. I was frozen in shock and dad didn't move from where he was standing. I was frightened for what was about to happen in this house.

"Have a good day at school" said my revengeful mom to her confused son. The door slammed and now dad was the victim of the most hideous stare I have ever seen from anyone, especially my mom.

I had no idea of what was building up inside mom now. "Kenton", she started, "you told me lie after lie. You looked me directly in my face and told me that you were NOT cheating on me. You didn't think about your children or me. Everybody in the neighborhood is talking about us now." She paused.

"I defended you because I felt there was NO way you could be out there desecrating our marriage. We took our vows for better or for worse. Not only did you cheat - but you got her PREGNANT. Not only did you get her PREGNANT, but now she calls you her FIANCE!"

One more pause.

"I didn't know you could HAVE a fiance if you're already MARRIED!"

The final word. Was dad digesting this, or fearing her reaction to all this? As mom spoke, she slowly walked to the coat closet and stooped down to pick up something. Then we saw it - KJ's baseball bat.

"Mom, what are you doing with that bat?" I intervened. I was scared for all of us. Nobody knew what she was capable of now. I remember the anger I unleashed on Cassandra and the damage I inflicted on her. Was mom capable of much worse damage? I didn't want to believe this was my mother in front of me now.

"Mom, please put down the bat," I pleaded. "Please don't do anything stupid. Dad is not worth you going to prison."

Mom continued to ignore me. She glared at dad while still speaking, but this time her voice descended to an evil octave and she started mumbling.

"I gave you 17 good years of marriage" she growled slowly to dad, "and through the good times and bad times, I stood by you. Not ONCE did I think about cheating on you." my dad stood up,

"Karla, I'm sorry, baby. I made a huge mistake. I didn't mean for this to happen...but I fell in love with her..."

Whack! Whack! Those words were all that were needed to cause the bat to become a weapon of mass destruction. The bat took a life of its own and started beating my dad, until he fell to the floor.

The beating continued. Now the bat made its way down to his legs. I couldn't take this anymore.

"Mom, STOP!" I yelled. "Please think about me and KJ, PLEASE! If you kill dad you will go to jail and we won't have anyone to take care of us!" I couldn't stop the torrent of tears as I pleaded with mom to stop beating dad. I was frantic now. I had to play the innocent child card.

I was scared. I could feel my mother's pain, but I didn't want her to kill my dad. Then all of a sudden, the beating ceased.

"Oh baby, I'm sorry" said an apologetic mother who just bashed her husband to the floor.

With that, she managed to get in three more swings before dropping the weapon. Then the tears flooded her eyes. I saw her run out of the house sobbing.

What does a child do in this situation? Does she run after her sobbing mother, or help her damaged father who just endured a vicious beating? I grabbed my phone and called 911 and described this horrific incident to the operator while we waited for an ambulance.

"Can you make sure he's breathing? Can you check his pulse and make sure he's still alive?" asked the operator.

I saw dad bleeding profusely on the floor. I checked his pulse and told the operator he was alive. The sirens were slowly approaching so I covered dad with a blanket in case he was going into shock, since he was losing a lot of blood. My thoughts now went to how I was going to describe this incident to the police. They were on their way and I knew I had to get my stories straight.

I didn't want my mother to end up in jail - I knew I had to stretch the truth.

I let EMS into the house and they stabilized dad. They praised me and told me I did a good job of taking care of him in the meantime. That praise was meaningless. If I really did a good job, dad would not be in this predicament. If I really did a good job as a daughter, we would all be sitting on the couch talking about our day. That would never happen again, as far as I could tell.

The police noticed how nervous and shaken I appeared when they arrived. Everything happened so fast I didn't know what was going to happen next. All I knew was that I had to protect my mom. There were a total of four police officers - two females and two males. One female office walked over to me and asked if I was okay.

"I'm a little shaken up. Is my dad going to be okay?" I asked.

"We don't know yet, but I assure you he is in good hands now." was the standard policy response I got.

At that point, two officers left and two officers remained. We really didn't need four officers adding to the confusion and stress in my opinion. I asked them if I could wash up because I had blood all over me.

"Sure, no problem". Another customary policy response.

I glanced at myself in the bathroom mirror. Who was this person looking back? The tears started rolling again. My life was over, and there was nothing I could do to fix it. Just a few days ago, I boasted of having the perfect family. Now I had evidence that this wasn't true. I was living a fantasy - what did I do to deserve this? I returned downstairs to the police officers after washing up.

"May I sit down?" asked one female officer.

"Sure" I replied, not caring if they sat or stood. I just wanted them gone.

"I'm Officer Roberts and my partner here is Officer Brown", she said. I was in no mood for cordial introductions. She then tells me they had a few questions to ask about the recent events.

"How old are you?" was the first question directed at me.

"I'm 15, but I'll be turning 16 in three days", I replied.

"Oh, happy early sweet 16", she replied back.

That response caused me and Officer Brown to both look at her strangely. How can she wish me a happily Sweet 16 given the gravity of the current moment?

She continued with her unassuming line of questioning. "Is it only you and your father who live here?"

"No", I replied, getting more frustrated by the minute. "It's my dad, my mom, my brother, and me".

"Oh", replied the Officer who I prayed would stop asking questions, "then where are your mom and brother now?"

I had to gather my thoughts. "My brother is at school and my mom is visiting my grandma, who is sick."

"Well, why aren't you in school, then?". Does she ever stop with the questions? How could her partner stand being around her, I wondered.

"Well, I was suspended because I was fighting a girl who wouldn't stop *bullying me*.". I made sure to emphasize the last part of that statement. I noticed Officer Roberts write down everything I said. Suddenly, it was Officer Brown's turn to speak.

"Can you tell us exactly what happened here?"

I decided to put on makeup as I started my response.

"I was upstairs in my bed when I heard a loud noise, So I jumped up and ran downstairs. I saw...a man standing over my dad with a silver bat. He dropped the bat and ran out the back door when he saw me. That's when I grabbed my cell phone and called you guys." I thought that was very plausible.

"Did you get a good look at the man standing over your dad?" asked Officer Roberts. I was content just speaking to Office Brown, but I had no control over who asked questions today.

"All I saw was what he was wearing, maybe part of his face. He was wearing a hoodie."

"Please try to remember anything about his clothes or about his face", the officers pleaded.

I couldn't. I was so overwhelmed. All I could do was dig deep into my memory and make this lie bigger. I started thinking about movie characters and pretending my fictional villain looked like them. The officers took my statement and then asked me if I called my mother.

"I didn't have a chance to call her, I wanted to make sure my dad was okay," was the best reply I could muster. They then told me to call my mom.

Why can't they just give me a break? I need a moment to take all this in? I dialed my mom's number. No answer. I didn't expect anyone to answer. I started praying silently that nothing bad happened to her. She was in very bad shape when she ran out of the house.

"She's not picking up", I told Officer Roberts.

"Is there anyone else you can call who can be with you now?" The Officers sounded concerned, but this was just another standard question from their playbook.

"No", I said bluntly, "but I would like to check on my dad."

They offered to drive me to the hospital, but first they had to wait for the crime scene technicians to arrive.

"Hey, why do you need the crime lab people to come?" I wondered out loud.

"Because your dad was a victim of a crime, they need to check for prints or DNA to catch whoever attacked your dad." More answers without real emotion. I felt like an episode of *Law & Order* was taking place right in my living room.

I started worrying about the lie I so easily concocted. I knew the crime lab nerds would ultimately find my mom's prints on the bat. How do I prepare for this revelation?

"Um, I just remembered the guy I saw had gloves on". Brilliant, that should hold them off.

"It doesn't matter, our guys still need to investigate this scene". My brilliance just crumbled onto the floor into a million pieces.

Ten minutes passed and the crime lab truck finally pulled up. The team entered the house, dusted for prints, took some samples, and then left. As promised, the two officers drove me to the hospital to see my dad.

I asked the nurse at the front desk if my dad was okay.

"Who's your dad, honey?" she asked

I gave her dad's name, and the nurse then said "Oh, he's in surgery for his femur. You can sit in the waiting area and I'll let you know when he's out of surgery."

I found the waiting area but I couldn't sit still. I paced the floor thinking about dad, mom, and KJ. Where would we all go from here? I didn't even notice that almost an hour and a half had already passed. Then I heard a voice in front of me.

"Hi, you must be the daughter. Your dad has a fractured skull, a few broken ribs and a fractured femur, which we did fix."

I felt the tears come down now. The damage was worse than I thought.

The doctor held my hand and tried to assure me that everything was going to be okay. "Your dad will make a full recovery. It's just going to take some time."

I was not reassured. Those were not the words I needed to hear right then.

"Can you take me to his room?" I asked softly. The doctor agreed.

I opened the door and saw dad lying there - his face and half of his body wrapped up. I started shaking, then I sat on one side of the bed and held his hand.

"I'm so sorry this happened", I said to him, quietly. "I wish I could make things better between you and mom."

I was hoping he heard those words. All I could do was lay my head on the bed and pray that everything would be okay. Then I heard the knock on the door.

"Come in". I had no idea who would be on the other side of that door. To my surprise, it was the infamous Dr. Ellis.

"What happened to your dad?" asked the man who the whole town was talking about now.

I couldn't answer him right away. All I could do was just stare at him. The silence didn't sit well with him, so he immediately turned his attention to my mom.

"Did your mom do this? Is she implicated in any way for this?" he asked.

That was the last straw. How dare this man push my buttons in my time of need.

I couldn't stop the barrage of words that poured out of my mouth. I was calling him all sorts of names, stuff I didn't even know I had in me.

"What's going on?" shouted Officer Roberts, who had just ran into the room when my mouth took a life of its own.

"I don't want to talk to this man", I said, pointing to the cause of my distress. "Please ask him to leave!"

Officer Roberts took my side and asked Dr. Ellis to leave. He slowly shuffled his feet in protest, so I gave it one more effort.

"GET OUT, NOW. GO!!" If I yelled any louder, the walls would have started shaking. Dr. Ellis finally vacated the room.

"Officer, I have to call my mom so she knows where I am".

I dialed my mom again. Again, no answer. But two seconds later, I heard a *ding*. Text message!

I hastily checked my text message and saw "What, Lexi?".

That's the text mom sent? Oh well, I had to reply to this.

I'm here at the hospital with dad, he's hurt really bad, I typed. I waited, then I saw the three little dots letting me know that she was replying. This was good - at least mom is responding. I didn't care how she responded, it could be by phone call, text message, or smoke signals. I just needed a live response. The text was almost done.

I don't care. I hope he dies.

This was the moment I knew I was losing both my parents. I had no energy to respond back to her. I was alone. I decided to text Kaylee.

Kaylee, can you pick up KJ from school so that he won't be alone?

Sure, she replied. I could always count on Kaylee, even when my world was quickly dissolving around me.

I stayed with my dad because nobody else was there with him. I propped my feet in the chair next to him and watched TV until I fell asleep. When I woke up, it was very dark outside. How long was I asleep? I quickly grabbed my phone hoping it was still charged. I noticed ten missed calls from Kaylee. I called her back.

"Hey, Lexi, I'm glad you called. I took KJ back to my house. When you leave the hospital, you can pick him up here."

I was groggy while she spoke. My head was throbbing and I decided to lay back in the chair and grab a few more minutes of sleep. Then my phone rang again. I thought Kaylee forgot to tell me something.

It was mom. She was on video now. I was not prepared for this. With my eyes half open, I answered the call.

"Lexi, I have something to show you", she said. Mom was sweating and tears were rolling down her face.

"Mom, are you....okay?", I couldn't believe what I was seeing.

"Lexi, mama is *not okay*". What did she mean by this?

"I'm so sorry this is happening so close to your birthday," she continued with the sweat growing by the minute. "You have become such a beautiful and courageous young lady, and I absolutely love you very much. But..." I hated that word, I always did. "I am tired of your stupid, jackass of a father hurting me like this!"

"Mom, what are you talking about?" I asked, hoping the sweat on her face would just stop.

"Lex, this has been going on for years. Your daddy has been cheating on me for years. I forgave him over and over again, and now, I'm finally - tired." That last word just died in midair. I could picture my mom collapsing after that final word. But she kept going. She turned the camera around and suddenly I noticed the lady who came to our house this morning - the *pregnant lady*.

"Mom, where are you?" I asked, concerned that something bad was about to happen.

"Is your dad awake?" asked my sweaty mom who was totally losing control on the other side of the camera lens.

"No, he's sleeping..."

"Wake him up..." she commanded.

"I can't do that, mom..."

"WAKE HIM UP, NOW!!" she yelled through the phone. I felt every patient in that hospital wake up after that last command.

I had no choice. I shook my dad and pleaded with him to wake up. He didn't move, so I shook harder. He finally opened his eyes. I put the camera in front of his damaged face.

"Kenton, I am fed up", said my mom. "When you give up a good thing for a *tramp* like this, you lose everything!" I saw the rage in my mother's eyes. "Not only did you *cheat* on me with her, you got her *pregnant* after I begged you to have another baby with me. You *proposed* to her, even though you were still married to me and had a family with *me*".

How long was this nightmare going to last? My dad needed rest and so did I. The rant continued.

"I forgave you time and time again, but it seems you can't teach an old dog a new trick. So..." I heard the tone get deeper and more wicked. "Since you brought her and her *bastard unborn child* into our lives, it's up to ME to take them out of It."

What? Who says things like that? This was not a movie I was watching, this was my mother! Who taught my mother to talk like this? Then we saw the disturbing image on the video call.

My mom slowly raised her hand and revealed a gun. A loaded gun, pointed at Jennifer's stomach. "Here's to 17 beautiful years together". The sight of the gun made my dad shuffle violently in bed. He tried forming words for mom, but the words were nowhere to be found. In their place were tears pouring from his eyes. As I watched dad struggle to speak, a bright flash of light followed by the sound of two gunshots filled the room. It was almost as if someone had shot both me and dad right there.

We both looked at the camera in horror, as Jennifer's head slowly fell towards the floor. The phone went dead and there was no movement in that hospital room. My perfect mother just ended four innocent lives on a video call - Jennifer, her unborn baby, dad, and me. How do we even tell Kaylee and KJ about this?

Chapter 5

"BLANK STARE"

It took a lot for me not to have a nervous breakdown at that moment. I thought to myself, "I'm only 15, I can't take care of KJ without mom and dad." After the video ended and the phone hung up, I looked over at my dad and he just looked back at me. If he could speak I'm sure the only words he would say were "Lex, I am so sorry, baby." It was better he didn't say anything.

I started pacing across the hospital room floor, trying to figure out my next step. Who could I call now? Even though my mom had gone way beyond the point of no return, I still didn't want her to get caught. After all, she is my *mother*. Was this a normal response I should be having? I have to leave this hospital room. I kissed my dad goodbye and called for a Lyft to take me to Kaylee's house. I had to figure out how to rescue my mom.

The Lyft finally reached Kaylee's house. I rang the doorbell. "Hi, Lexi. My goodness, you don't look so good, what is going on?" asked Kaylee's mom.

"I was visiting a family member in the hospital and it was sort of emotional". I was getting very good at fictionalizing life now.

"I'm so sorry to hear this", she said. "We are here for your family whenever you need us".

I thanked her for these comforting words, then immediately looked for Kaylee and KJ. I saw KJ sitting on the bed watching TV, calm as ever. I had to tell Kaylee what happened, in private, away from KJ's innocent ears.

"Kaylee, can KJ please spend the night here? I have to do damage control with my mom."

"Lexi, I need to come with you to watch your back. I want to make sure everything is okay."

Kaylee really wanted to be with me now, so her mom agreed to keep an eye on KJ.

We hopped in the car and started driving away. When we reached the first stoplight, a very familiar looking car pulled up beside us. I casually glanced to my right and saw my mom. *Oh my God, she can't see me now.* Mom's bloodied hands were gripping the steering wheel and her hair was a mess. She appeared in a cold, lifeless daze, totally unrecognizable. When she tried to look in my direction, I quickly crouched down in my seat and told Kaylee to follow her at a safe distance behind. I didn't want mom to know she was being followed.

We drove for about ten minutes before mom pulled into a gas station. We saw her carry a large red container which she was mindlessly filling up with gas. We both stared and wondered why mom would need this large container of gas. The container was topped off and placed back into the trunk of mom's car. She drove off and we continued tailing her. A few minutes later, we saw her pull into the parking lot of dad's office.

The office was opened even though dad was lying in the hospital. Three other doctors worked in the same building and that's why the lot was packed full of cars now. What could mom be doing here at this time of day?

Both me and Kaylee started thinking the same horrible thought.

"Please tell me she is not about to do what I *think* she's about to do," I said out loud.

As soon as I said that, mom slowly exited the car with a ski mask over her face and a hoodie over her head. Her only focus was the canister of gas in the trunk.

"Mommy, please. What are you doing?" I screamed as I ran towards her in fear. "Why are you acting like this?"

"Alexis, get OUT OF MY WAY", she yelled at me.

"Mom, I can't do that. I know you're hurting, but we can FIX this. Please. Just STOP all this craziness and come home to me and KJ," I begged her.

At that point the mask on her head came up and she gave me the coldest stare I ever received in my short life.

"It's too late!" she said slowly. You better leave, before I MAKE you". My mom never threatened me before. Ever. I had no idea what that meant, but I knew it wasn't good. I mustered enough courage and tried to pull that red canister away from her. We struggled back and forth for what seemed an eternity until I felt a huge pain in my head.

My own mother hit me in the head with the same gun she used to kill Jennifer.

I fell to the ground in so much pain. I felt everything around me start to spin. As I laid on the ground I saw her determined feet move towards the medical office. She reached the stairs outside and poured gasoline everywhere she could. Then I heard the front door open as she carried her evil soul over the threshold, like a groom carrying his bride on their wedding day.

Kaylee ran to my side when she saw me on the ground. I leaned on her as we walked towards the building. I was still dizzy from the blunt force I received. I noticed blood coming from my head, but I didn't care. All I cared about was my mom and whatever she was doing on the other side of that door. Two minutes passed and then we heard it.

Bang. Bang. Bang. Bang!

I didn't want to hear any more gunshots. Ever. The two I heard on the video call were enough. And now four more shattered my fragile existence. We both ran towards the building and tried to glance through the double glass doors to see what had just happened. We saw mom - standing over the receptionist desk with her gun pointing downward. She had just shot Brandy. We saw a waiting room full of patients. I had to act.

"Mom, let these people go! They have nothing to do with this!" I yelled as I ran inside.

Mom looked at me and raised her gun. I had a gun pointed at me.

"Lexi, I told you to LEAVE! I am now going to count to three. If you're NOT gone by then, I am going to shoot my own daughter!"

I was warned. I was scared. What mother, in her right mind, would point a gun at her 15-year old daughter? Even if not in her right mind, I am her 15-year old daughter!

"1..." the countdown already began.

"Mom, please..." I pleaded between counts.

"2..." she continued.

"Mom, at least let the children go!" I quickly used the innocent-child card to thwart her evil intentions.

Suddenly, mom looked around and noticed how scared the kids were in that waiting room. She motioned for all the kids to leave, so I grabbed them and pushed them towards Kaylee, who slowly walked them outside while I continued negotiating with my mom.

I told her that it wasn't too late for us to leave together and run away. But all mom said was, "3" and then she moved closer towards me. I backed up slowly out the door and down the stairs. Somehow I knew that if I didn't leave she would have shot me - her own daughter. I ran to Kaylee's car and then I heard six loud shots. Then my mom ran out like a scared animal. She poured the remaining gas from the canister near the building entrance and all over the stairs.

I heard the police sirens and then wondered who actually called them. Mom also heard the sirens and ran to the bottom of the stairs. She carefully removed two matches from a small box and struck them against the side. I saw the small canons of fire arch gracefully through the air as it landed on the stairs, setting off a blaze of destruction. Mom then drove off like a lightning bolt leaving horrible skid marks and eternal nightmares behind her.

I glanced at the building and saw flames everywhere. There was a loud blast that shook the ground, causing me to grab Kaylee and run as we dived into the safety of our car. I hated leaving those innocent children behind, but I knew that the cops would soon be on the scene. I turned to Kaylee and started screaming at the top of my lungs.

"What did my mom just do? *Please* tell me she didn't just *kill* all of those innocent people!" Kaylee could see the blood boiling inside of me. My mom had officially become a mass *murderer*. She took innocent lives and I no longer had any respect for her.

Chapter 6

"ON THE RUN"

After witnessing my mother killing all those innocent people, I felt traumatized. I kept reminding myself of her horrific acts because now it was all over the news. To make matters worse, Kaylee and I were not the only witnesses. Two other people saw my mom take off her mask in the parking lot of my dad's office building, right before she hit me with the gun.

Since we live in a small town everybody practically knew who my mom was. That meant they knew *us* as well. I'm sure that by this time my mom knew she was wanted for murder. That meant she was on the run. Yet I had a strange feeling she was going to show up soon. The murders had reached the level of national news, so even my grandparents had seen what was happening. I noticed dozens of calls from my grandma on my phone. She obviously didn't know what caused mom to snap like she did, but she desperately wanted to know how all this could have been prevented.

I called grandma and told her that it was too much to explain over the phone. The one thing I knew about grandma was that she never gave up, ever. She repeated that she wanted the whole story between mom and dad and then told me she would be in town later that evening.

"Everything is going to be okay", I reassured her, "You don't have to come, I'll keep you posted."

"Don't be a foolish child", said grandma sternly, "I have to be there for you and KJ."

I had no strength to argue. "Okay, grandma, we'll see you soon". Click. The phone hung up.

I was very nervous about grandma coming to see us - who knows what mom is capable of now? Who else is mom going to point that gun at and.... shoot? Mom told me she loved me, then she hits me over the head with... that gun? Karla Samuels would *never* do that. My mom was no longer Karla Samuels. She was now a woman scorned - and fed up - and there was nothing anyone could do about it.

I needed a distraction to occupy my mind, so I started cleaning the house to prepare for grandma's arrival. I kept cleaning until nothing remained to be cleaned. The whole house sparkled. I suddenly realized that I wish I could make my life sparkle in the same way. I ran upstairs to fix the guest room so grandma could be as comfortable as possible, considering all the chaos going on. My phone rang like it was in pain. I heard Kaylee's voice.

"Hey, turn on the tv, hurry up", she said.

"What channel, what's going on?" I asked, stunned.

"It doesn't matter, it's breaking news all over the place, on every station!"

I felt like I couldn't move, but I forced my feet downstairs and switched the tv on to Channel 8, our usual source of truth. My eyes were glued on the caption MURDER SUSPECT KARLA SAMUELS HOLDS POLICE OFFICER HOSTAGE. Was there hope for my mom, after all the things she did? My heart kept saying "Yes". But the news was saying "No". I saw a live news feed outside Chandler's supermarket where mom always buys her groceries. Why would mom go to the grocery story knowing she was wanted for murder?

I had a million thoughts in my head, but one thought ran to the front of the line - Maybe the reason she was there was that nobody there suspected it was her who killed Brandy and all those innocent people and then set the doctor's office building on fire. The tv anchor described how mom was robbing the store, then shot an off-duty cop in the leg when he tried to subdue her. After shooting him, she took some hostages - five people that they could account for.

More thoughts started appearing out of nowhere.

If mom has money, then why rob a grocery store?

Then I noticed the purse by the coat rack. There's my answer - she needs money. I looked back at the TV and noticed almost a dozen cop cars and one long black SUV that just pulled up. *FBI*. This just got real, I told myself. My mom is now surrounded by the *FBI*. Then I noticed a sniper on a roof across from the grocery store.

"There is now a sniper with orders to shoot when he has the target in sight".

FBI. Snipers. My mom was the target. I lost Karla Samuels somewhere between my 15th and 16th birthday. I was terrified.

My body took over. I suddenly realized my mother was about to die. How could she possibly escape the FBI or the sniper? I had to figure a way to help her. I didn't care how extreme my plan was. I called Kaylee and asked her to pick me up "because I needed help with something.". Without hesitation, Kaylee complied.

I ran to my mom's room and grabbed a BB gun belonging to dad from the top shelf closet. It was a long black gun with a scope. I remember how dad and I used to shoot cans in the backyard with this gun, what we called father-daughter bonding. I then opened my phone and sent a text to mom telling her to wait for another text. It said, *When you get this next text, please MOVE to the back of the store.*

Mom texted back - *what are you doing, Lex?*

I had to tell her - *Mom, you're all over the news, there are SNIPERS outside waiting for a clear view to KILL YOU! I am trying to HELP YOU!*

There was silence for three seconds. Then these words:

I don't want you to get involved. Please stay away!

I could not stay away. I replied back - *No matter what you did, you are still my mom! I still love you!*

I wonder if I meant those words. Even though I had little to no respect for her, I still loved her.

Thank you, she texted back'

Don't thank me yet! I replied. I wondered why I had texted those words.

Then I heard Kaylee on the phone. She was waiting for me outside. I quickly put on some black jeans, black boots, a black hoodie and my Michael Kors sunglasses, then ran downstairs. I saw dozens of news trucks in front of our house and every neighbor staring intently at this chaos. There was Ms. Jackson, the Rona Barrett of the neighborhood, speaking with Channel 6 News. What a sight this was.

Then all eyes were upon me. I could see the whole neighborhood rush towards me.

"I'm sorry", I shot back, "I'm only 15 years old and I can't say anything without my mom or dad here."

That wasn't good enough. One newswoman badgered me with questions, but I had no answers to give.

"Is it true your mother stole medication from her workplace and consumed it all, which made her go crazy?"

I wanted to punch this newsperson in the face so hard, but I had bigger fish to fry. I managed to push her to the ground and reach the safety of Kaylee's car. Kaylee sped off and we drove to the same building that KJ and I used to play in when mom took us to the grocery store as little kids.

"Lex, you do know that KJ was crying all night when he saw your mom's picture on the news", she told me while keeping her eyes on the road.

I simply shook my head, I had nothing to say in return. But I knew deep down I had to take care of KJ somehow. We saw the building approaching and I asked Kaylee to circle the block a few times and wait for my call. I got out of the car and ran into the building. I sent another text to mom and told her to start backing up slowly towards the back door exit.

Okay, she texted back. She was on her way to the rear entrance.

I lifted the BB gun and pointed it towards the cops stationed in front of the store. Please God, forgive me, I prayed silently. My right eye was on top of the scope and then I pulled the trigger. Cops were running and ducking for cover. I grabbed my phone in one hand and left the gun in my other hand. I called mom and told her to RUN. I stared through the window and saw her running through some bushes behind the store. All I could do was keep shooting to give her a good lead. When she was finally out of sight, I dialed Kaylee to pick me up. No answer. Ten more times. No answer.

I was alone. I was on my own now. What happened to Kaylee? This was not like her, she was always there for me. Frantically I decided to run up four flights of stairs. I wrapped the BB gun inside my hoodie and dropped it inside a trash bin near a door labeled "*Suga's magic room*". I snuck inside and was told to leave. After telling a stranger I was being chased by someone dangerous, he took me inside to a break room in the back.

"Stay here, I'll be right back", he said.

I desperately searched for some way out of there - a window, a door, any opening. But there was no way out. I sat down at a large white table for what seemed like eternity. Where would I go from here? I noticed a strange handle on the floor and suddenly my curiosity piqued. Where does that lead to? I've seen handles like this all the time in the movies. Was this a movie handle? In the movies, this always meant a trap door. Would I be so lucky now?

Then I heard the stranger tell the cops at the front door that I was being chased. I had to act quickly. I pulled that handle as hard as I could. The first time, nothing. The second time, nothing. Then I grabbed the red broom in the corner and pried it open after the third attempt. I jumped in and closed the trap door behind me. I saw stairs going downward from the entrance. I slowly made my way to the bottom and then held my breath. I wish I never came down here.

I saw dozens of old men with young models types , all wearing lingerie or bathing suits of some type.

I sneaked around carefully, making sure nobody saw me. I finally noticed a door leading out of the building. I walked outside and then ran into the same woods I saw my mom go through. While I ran, I tripped over a big stone used for sitting. This hurt my ankle really bad. I could barely walk after that, so I just laid there hoping somebody would find me. After laying there for quite some time - I didn't even know what time it was - I heard something shuffling in the grass on my left side. It was mom! I couldn't believe it!

"Lex, are you okay", she whispered to me.

"I hurt my ankle, it hurts when I walk", I whispered back.

She wrapped my arms around her shoulders and lifted me off the grass. I couldn't believe my eyes. Mom walked slowly as I limped in pain. Almost a mile later we both noticed a very old rusted house just ahead of us. It was completely abandoned.

We approached the house and out of nowhere appeared a wrinkled old lady with gray hair, wearing a long white and blue floral night dress, just sitting on the porch.

"Excuse me, ma'am, could you please help my daughter?" asked mom. "She hurt her ankle and can barely walk".

The old lady just stared at mom and then shouted, "Aren't you that lady who's all over the news? The one who killed all those people?"

My mom didn't respond. She guided me to the last stair and set me down. I reached into my pocket, took out my phone and removed my debit card from the case.

"Here, mom. Take this and run as far away as possible".

Mom looked at me for a whole minute then kissed me on my forehead. She turned around and was gone.

The old lady then helped me up the stairs and placed me on the oldest couch I ever saw. My feet were elevated on her deck table. She brought me some wrapping bandages, ice, and something she called witch hazel. I felt this strange ointment being rubbed all over my hurt ankle.

"Was that lady really your mother?" asked my strange new caretaker.

"Yes, ma'am", I replied, happy to have someone tend to my aching ankle.

"What would cause your mother to do something so...vile?" said the old lady.

"Her husband." My reply was short and sweet.

"Say no more. Child, I had one of *those* for almost 40 years. I was so happy when he died, mm hmm. He passed right there in that chair on this porch." There was no emotion on her face.

This creeped me out. I had to excuse myself to make a phone call.

"Sure, baby. Take your time". Nothing she said made me feel calm.

I called Kaylee again, but still got no answer. Now I was flooded with worry. Did something happen to Kaylee also? There was no time for this extra worry. I had to get back home before grandma arrived. I tried to order a Lyft but no available drivers in the area so I booked an On Demand ride and my driver was just three minutes away. Thank God I stored my debit card number on the app. After the car arrived, I yelled to the old lady to inform her I was leaving. I thanked her for the witch hazel.

"Come back anytime, it gets lonely here" said the old lady. I was hoping this was the last time we ever met.

"Thank you, ma'am, I sure will". I lied to her. I was getting better and better at lying.

"Enough of that ma'am stuff, honey. Call me Ms. Ruth".

"Yes ma'am...I mean ....Ms. Ruth" I said while Ms. Ruth walked me to the vehicle. I waved at her as we drove off.

We finally reached my destination and the On Demand driver pulled me out with my back facing him. We both walked to the front door and I assured him I would be okay.

"Thank you, sir," I told the Good Samaritan.

"No need to thank me, it's my job. Imagine how many drunk people I get to drive home and help into their houses. I have no problem helping a beautiful young lady like yourself."

"Uh, could I use your bathroom? I really need to go."

How could I turn down someone who went the extra mile helping me in this condition?

"Sure, it's the least I can do", I told him. I pointed him to the bathroom and then called grandma to check on her flight. No luck, the call went straight to voicemail, so she must still be in flight. I was exhausted now so I laid my head on the couch and closed my eyes for a few seconds. Then I heard the front door screen slam shut. I jumped and opened my eyes. Was it the Lyft driver? How could he leave and not say goodbye? Oh well, it doesn't matter.

I felt my mouth become very dry. I hopped off the couch and limped to the kitchen for a drink. As soon as I pulled the juice bottle from the fridge, I felt a large hand wrap around my mouth. Another large hand held me from behind. What was happening? I started to scream and shuffle. Who was doing this to me? My screams were muffled by this large hand over my mouth. I dropped the juice and used my free hand to scratch whoever was standing behind me. I scratched hard.

The person let go for a few seconds and I crawled to the living room as fast as I could, without even checking behind me. The room was dark but I remembered where dad hid his knife collection. I reached for the biggest knife I could grab. I managed to turn around and I saw a very tall shadow approach me. I pointed the knife and in my strongest voice I said, "Do not come any closer." But the shadow kept approaching closer to me. A small speck of light shone into the kitchen from the living room, illuminating this shadow for a few seconds. It was the On demand driver!

"What are you doing?" I asked him, in shock.

"I had to come back for you" he replied with a low, dangerous tone.

I didn't understand this. "What are you talking about?" I asked him.

"You are SO beautiful and I think I'm in love with you", he said using his sinister voice.

That's when fear gripped me. I was confused.

"You just MET me, you only gave me ONE ride. And now you LOVE me?"

"I know, I know. But haven't you ever heard of love at first sight?" he asked?

"Look, I'm only 15 years old. You can't do this!" I screamed back.

The shadow just looked at me. "But you have the body of a goddess. Age ain't nothing but a number, honey. The younger, the better. Less drama, right?"

I was still pointing the large knife directly at him. "Please leave, you're really scaring me, sir"

"Why are you calling me *sir*? Please don't do that! We are *soulmates*!" he said.

This was getting creepier and creepier by the minute.

I started shaking and then put my head down for a second. The driver grabbed the knife from my hand and threw it behind him. I grabbed the umbrella near me and hit him with it while I was still on the floor. I tried to crawl away, but he grabbed my bad ankle and pulled me towards him. He then ripped off my shirt and started unbuttoning my pants. I tried to kick back, but my ankle felt like it was broken, so I tried to kick back with my good foot. It didn't even phase him, because he kept pushing harder. I screamed as loud as I could. I was hoping this was the one time our nosey neighbor Ms. Jackson would hear me.

While he was on top of me, I tried to fight him off. But he was way too strong and he simply overpowered me. He then pulled his pants down and forced himself inside me. I felt so much pain in that moment, and all I could do was cry and lay there on the floor. After he finished, he told me he loved me and he was happy that we were together. I was living nightmare after nightmare and didn't have time to process any of this. When will it end?

The driver got up and headed to the kitchen. I just laid on the floor with my pants and underwear down to my ankles, crying uncontrollably. I was in so much pain. The man came back to where I was laying and started to wipe tears away from my face.

"Why are you crying, baby? Didn't that feel good? You know I'm going to love you forever, right?" he said to me.

I stared at him and all I could see was blackness in his eyes as he stared back at me with a huge smile on his face.

"Police, show me your hands and get on the ground" were the next words I heard. I felt relief for a second and internally thanked nosey Ms. Jackson for calling the cops, even though the cavalry came a little later than I hoped. I saw this evil man being handcuffed and led out of our house. A female officer helped me get my clothes on. I cried on her shoulder.

"I need to take a shower" I told her.

"Wait, did this man touch you in your...private parts?" she asked.

I broke down and fell into her arms. "He raped me," I replied.

The officer held me in her arms and said, "I'm so sorry, sweetheart. I have to call an ambulance to take you to the hospital now."

"Why do I have to go to the hospital?" I asked.

"Anytime a person is a victim of rape, we have to do something called a rape kit", she explained.

I pictured myself saying "no" but instead, I told the officer I didn't want anyone to take me to the hospital, except for her. She grabbed my hand.

"Where are your clothes?" she asked me. I pointed her to my upstairs bedroom. "Second door on the left", I replied. She ran upstairs to retrieve a shirt for me. When she came back down, she had a quizzical look on her face. "Who's the man in the pictures hanging in the hallway?" she inquired.

"That's my dad. Do you know him?"

"We'll talk later. Let's get you to the hospital", she shot back. She noticed my ankle and allowed me to lean on her as we walked to the car.

"Why did you ask me about my dad?" I asked her.

The office started the car and didn't speak for a few minutes. Then came a response which proved my life would become more complicated with each passing day.

"I don't think you would believe me if I told you", she started.

"Hey, the way my life has been going lately, I would believe *anything* you tell me" I countered back. I really meant that also.

"Okay", she sighed, "Well...long story short. You...are my little sister. I knew it as soon as I saw that picture -"

I wanted to yell but I just stared up at the blank sky. God somehow felt I could handle one shock after another. I looked at her and my mouth opened so wide I thought it would never be shut closed again. How could this be possible?

"How?" I had to repeat that word out loud just to be sure everyone heard it except me.

"Your dad and my mom dated when they were 15", the officer started slowly. "They broke up because your grandma forbid them from seeing each other after they were caught having sex in her room one day." The image of that made me uncomfortable.

"My mom said she had never seen your dad again, " the officer continued. "A month later, she found out she was pregnant with me. I joined the police force at 20, and I'm 24 now. After 3 years of crazy crime in New Orleans, I needed something less chaotic. So I searched online and I noticed that this small town was looking for officers. I applied to the force and here I am - transferred three weeks ago." I always knew who my dad was, I just never searched for him. I have pictures of him and his siblings that Grandma Novey gave me from a party a few years back.

My small brain couldn't handle this. I laid back in my seat and processed the recent events that transpired in sequence, as best as I could.

So...my father cheated on my mother...now he's in the hospital because my mother almost killed him. My mother killed multiple people and then burned down the building with people still inside. My mother is now on the run, and now I discover I have an older sister. And, oh yes, I was just raped by a mad man.

Did I leave anything out? Can it get any worse than this? Was this some sort of test from God? If so, I am definitely failing with no chance of passing!

Chapter 7

"Far From Over"

As I lie in this hospital bed, a complete stranger takes swabs of my private area, and I just ponder how disgusted I feel. My bottom area feels so much pain and discomfort. I couldn't believe that I had been raped just one day before my 16th birthday...*Why me out of all people?* I started to think about my life up to this point. I knew that I wasn't doing all the "right things" lately, but for most of my 15 years of life, I have been a good person! Why, then, I rationalized, why were all these bad things happening to me now? I felt there would never be a good answer to this question and that made me even more depressed.

After the nurse finished with her rape kit and exam, she told me to get dressed. After a few minutes, I heard a knock on the door.

"Who is it?" I asked anxiously.

"Dr. Ellis." The voice made me freeze - I did not want to see Dr. Ellis, especially now.

"Go away, please," I yelled, trying to be polite at the same time.

"Please, Alexis, it's about your dad." At the mention of my dad, I ran to the door and opened it.

"What's going on with my dad?" I inquired.

"Please sit down for a minute," he started. I decided to just let his words flow without any preparation.

"Alexis, I'm so sorry, but your dad suffered a heart attack. The doctors tried to do everything they could, but he passed away an hour ago."

This had to be a joke. Those words crushed me like an old car at the junkyard. My legs just buckled and I fell straight into the arms of Dr. Ellis. I started crying so hard that I lost my voice. The only thought I had was that *while I was being raped, my father was dying*. I thought I had hit rock bottom, but somehow my bottom didn't have a floor. I finally knew what "bottomless" felt like. I had no life left in me.

I forced the next question from my lungs. "Dr. Ellis, can you take me to my dad?"

We walked down a long dim hallway, passing Officer Erica - my new sister. Erica saw the tears well up in my eyes. "What's wrong?" she asked.

I couldn't answer. I started crying even harder.

"My daddy is gone..." I muttered unintelligibly.

"WHAT? HOW?" was Erica's shocked reply.

I didn't have the strength to tell her everything but I promised to reveal everything to her later.

"Where are you going now?" she asked me.

"To see him" I said without looking at her. I needed someone there with me, besides Dr. Ellis, and Kaylee was nowhere to be found. I grabbed Erica's hand and we continued down the dimly lit hall together. My ankle was still in pain so I held onto Erica tightly. .

I was getting weaker and weaker, the closer we got to where Dad was laying. I felt my legs buckle and my hands shaking. We finally reached the room where my father was laid, and I noticed three officers standing at the door. Dr. Ellis told one officer I was "the daughter", after which I was told to go in as long as I "didn't touch anything".

"I need Officer Erica to come in with me," I told the officer. We both entered the room.

Why were the police here if my dad only had a heart attack? I wondered. I asked Erica to ask the other officer about this also. When she returned to the bed, she told me my dad had a heart attack because of injuries sustained while my mom attacked him. That's why it suddenly became a murder investigation.

"What happened to your dad?" asked Erica.

I couldn't tell her now, so I delayed my response. I walked up to dad's bed

Officer Erica asked me what happened to my dad? I told her again that I would tell her later. I walked up to my dad's bed and just stared at him. He looked so peaceful in that moment. Why does it take *death* to make people feel peaceful? Why can't people be this peaceful during *life?* All this chaos was turning me into a philosopher of sorts. I thought about mom. Was there a chance that she still loved and cared for dad, despite all that she had done to him?

"Officer Erica, I'm so sorry you had to meet dad like this. He was a great father and heart surgeon. And up until a few days ago, I *thought* he was a great husband also!"

Erica rubbed dad's hand for a minute.

"Hi daddy, I'm *so sorry* we didn't get a chance to meet when you were alive, but I *promise you* that I will be here for my little sister and brother. Don't worry about anything. Just be free and fly high!" Suddenly tears gushed from her eyes. Erica was so emotional at that point that she ran out of the room.

I felt coldness in the air as I continued to look at my dad. I glanced over at the table where his food was sitting and I saw my mom's watch given to her by grandma. I smiled. At least mom visited dad before he died. But wait - didn't my mom tell me she hoped dad *would die?* My mind began to race - *did mom come back to finish the job? I told her to run. Why would she come back here?*

I couldn't let that watch sit there forever. I hopped to the table on my good foot and grabbed the watch, hoping that nobody would notice it was gone. I then hopped back to my dad's bed to lay a final kiss on his forehead. "I love you and I will miss you" were my final words to him. Then I hopped out of the room and saw Erica.

"Officer Erica, can you take me to see my little brother?" I asked. Erica wiped her face and agreed. She quickly told her captain, "I have an emergency, I need to take off the rest of the day. Please clock me out, I'll stop by the station later."

I really wanted her to know what happened to our father, she deserved to know this. While we drove to Kaylee's house, I decided to confide in her and tell her *everything*. All this news shocked her - a higher state of shock than when I first heard she was my sister. She had so many questions, naturally.

"Where is your mom?" was the first question that came out.

Should I tell her this information? I had so many trust issues now - I definitely was NOT going to divulge this to her. What if she was playing me somehow? Could I really trust her?

"I don't know, honestly", was my reply.

"What are you going to do, now that both your mom and dad are gone?"

I had no idea what I was going to do. Nobody prepared me for this moment.

The phone rang - it was grandma.

"Hey Lexi, I'm at the house but nobody is here," she said.

"Grandma, I'm picking up KJ from a friend's house, I'll be home soon."

Grandma knew we had been through a lot these past few days.

"I'll make you a good meal when you get here". This was a standard grandmother reply to any situation. We pulled up to Kaylee's house and I limped to the front door.

"Heyy Lexi, I was wondering where you girls were," said Kaylee's mom as she opened the door.

"Wait, Kaylee's not home?" I asked her.

"No", she said. "The last time I saw her, she told me you both had something special to do."

"Oh, yeah. We did". I had to think on my feet. "I remember. She said she was going to Candace's house to ask her dad about some job he was hiring for."

Kaylee's mom was surprised at that statement. "Ok, honey", she smiled. She was definitely not convinced with my impromptu answer. I actually didn't know where Kaylee was, but I was praying she was okay, no matter what. I had to come up with a white lie to her mom *just in case* Kaylee was at her boyfriend's house.

"Where's KJ?" I asked, hoping to divert attention away from Kaylee. After hearing his name, KJ ran out the door and into my arms. I got the biggest hug in my life.

"I am so happy to see you, have you found mom yet?" said my anxious little brother. "I heard on the news that mom is on the run. All our neighbors were saying what a good woman mom is, except Ms. Jackson, of course." This produced a little chuckle but nothing could replace the true feelings inside of me.

"I haven't seen mom yet, but hopefully she will come back soon. Grandma is in town and she's waiting for us at home now."

KJ dragged me to the car when he heard that and I had to remind him about my broken ankle. The dragging stopped when he heard that.

"Are we in trouble?" he suddenly asked me.

"Why do you think we're in trouble?" I asked him. I was curious why he even thought that.

"Look." He pointed to the police car. I laughed.

"We're not in trouble. Officer Erica just wants to make sure that we get home safely, that's all."

"Ohh okay" he smiled. "I call shotgun".With that, KJ occupied the front seat and I was forced to sit in the back of the police car. The thought occurred to me that I chose this seat *voluntarily*. I hope I never see the day when I am *forced* to sit in the back of a police car - in handcuffs!

My little brother was in heaven in the front seat.

"Officer, can you turn on the sirens?" he asked. Oh my god, really?

Erica smiled and said, "Sure, little man." Oh please, don't humor *him*, I thought. KJ was now turning the siren off and on and scaring every driver on that road.

"Hey, little brother, chill out, man", I said, trying to calm my nerves.

I thought that would quiet KJ down, but I was wrong. The questions kept coming out of his mouth in rapid-fire succession. How do I pull the plug on this?

"Did you kill anyone?" was question number one. Erica responded "No".

"Do you like being a cop?" was question number two. "It has its good days and bad days," she replied honestly.

"How many people have you arrested?" was question number three. Seriously, does anyone keep track of this number? Is it even important?

"A billion", joked Erica. She sounded so convincing with that number.

"Word? That's lit," was my brother's street-gang reply. He was trying to be so cool in the moment.

Erica laughed. "I never heard anybody tell me that arresting people was *lit*. I never met anyone like you".

I stared at the occupants of the front row. It was almost as if KJ was *flirting* with Erica.

"Hey, KJ, slow your roll," I cautioned him from my perch in the back row.

"Stop being such a *hater*," he said as he glared at me from his first-class seat. That made me laugh and forget all the chaotic crap going on in my life, but I quickly snapped back into reality when I heard the next question from my inquisitive little pain-in-the-neck.

"How's dad doing?" This question made time stand still in that squad car.

Erica looked at me in the rear view mirror. I shook my head back and forth, signaling her to not say anything.

"I don't know right now, but when I find out, I will let you guys know". Good answer, Erica.

Then KJ wrote down something on a piece of paper he grabbed from his backpack. He handed the paper to Erica.

"Call me first when you hear anything," he told her. Then he winked at her. I could not believe KJ was giving his phone number to Erica.

"You must be one little player," she told him, as she smiled and shook her head jokingly.

"No, the ladies just love me," said my flirtatious little brother.

We arrived home and KJ jumped out and grabbed my crutch to help me out.

"Officer Erica, please come in and stay for dinner," I asked, hoping for a positive response. I could tell Erica was apprehensive about what grandma may say to her, but I assured her there was nothing to be nervous about.

"Grandma, we're home," I yelled as we entered the house. I heard a voice from upstairs.

"I'll be down in a minute". While KJ got ready for dinner, I limped over to the couch. After a few minutes of sitting, I gazed at the spot where I was raped. My mind flashed back and I could visualize myself getting raped all over again. The memory was vivid and I kept replaying this in my mind. I saw the mad man take off my pants and put his *thing* inside of me. It was like an out-of-body experience. I was telling my past memory to fight back, but the girl on the floor was just laying there, allowing this to happen. I allowed this to happen.

"Alexis, are you alright?" Erica's voice caused me to snap out of my recollection.

"Yeah, I'm good," I told her.

"Listen, if you ever need to talk, I'm here for you. Believe it or not, I know *exactly* what you're going through."

That made me more upset.

"How in the world can you know what I'm going through?" Erica could see the anger swell up inside me. "Are you *me*? Can *you* feel the pain I have down there? Huh?!"

"Alexis, calm down", she started. "Listen, the real reason I transferred to this little town's police force was because of something that happened to me earlier. I was on patrol in a really rough neighborhood on Desire

Street. I heard a loud scream, so I went to check it out. I saw this young girl being raped by two guys wearing hoodies."

I thought that would be the end of the story, but there was more.

"I froze. All I could focus on was the young girl's face," she continued. "The girl was crying and screaming for me to help. I pulled out my gun and told the two suspects to freeze and step away from her. One of them started cussing and said I didn't have the balls to pull the trigger. I shot my gun just to scare him and it didn't hit him."

Erica paused, signifying this story would get worse.

"I called for backup and before I knew it, someone hit me from behind. I fell to the ground and was semi-conscious. One suspect ripped off my clothes and raped me, and then another, and then another..." She started crying at that point. "I lost count after the fifth guy. I blacked out and when I came to, I was in the hospital. My captain told me I had been gang-raped and they only caught two of the eight guys who raped me."

She paused to take a breath, not looking directly at me.

"That was the worst day of my life - not only was I a victim of a gang rape, I was also told I couldn't have children because of my internal injuries. A few months later, I tested positive for HIV."

Suddenly, my pain couldn't compare to her pain. But we were both victims and we were both helpless. There was no room for comparison. I felt very close to her at that moment but I didn't say anything.

"So you see, little sis," Erica continued after describing this horrific story, "I *do know* what you're going through. You're a victim. I know you want to be strong, but the reality is, you're hurting. This won't go away until you deal with it. Talk to someone, find a counselor. That's how I was able to move forward and continue my duties as a police officer."

My eyes were filled with tears - I could literally feel her pain as she told her story. I hugged her tightly, knowing that this hug would benefit both her and me. I also needed to be comforted in the moment.

"What's going on?" asked Grandma as she noticed me hugging Officer Erica. I asked my grandma to sit next to me on the couch and gave her the same hug I offered Erica. I then told her everything I knew. I could see the pained look on Grandma's face. She held my face in her hands and looked directly into my eyes.

"Lexi, I'm *so sorry* you're going through all of this, sweetheart. I want you to know that I will be here with you through everything. You are *not alone.*"

"Thank you, grandma. I love you so much," was all I could say then.

"Officer Erica, someone is outside parked in a dark black car," said KJ, appearing out of nowhere.

Erica slowly got up and told everyone to get on the floor. KJ crawled over to where all of us were laying. Erica grabbed her gun from her holster and turned off the lights. She walked to the door and stared out the peephole.

"Be quiet, everyone," she whispered. We could see her silhouette behind the door with a raised gun in the air. The door creaked open and an unknown presence walked in. We had no idea who this was.

The lights came on suddenly and Erica pointed a loaded gun at the intruder. It was Laurence.

"WAIT, I know him," I shouted, before Erica had the chance to shoot. Erica lowered her weapon and turned toward Laurence.

"Why were you sitting outside in a dark car?" she quizzed him.

"I borrowed my dad's car to come and check on Lex," he said calmly. "I didn't hear from her, and I saw Lex's mom on the news. I wanted to make sure she was okay."

"Laurence, I'm fine, don't worry..."

My sentence was broken by another sound from the back door. Erica immediately turned after pushing Laurence on the floor and walked towards the door. She stood with her gun drawn again. Everything seemed like a scene from the movies. It was almost as if Erica had rehearsed this move a hundred times before. The door opened.

"What are YOU doing here?" I yelled to our new intruder, Mrs. Karen, Dr. Ellis' wife.

"Wait, you know *her* too?" Erica asked me in disbelief. Why were all these people coming to the house today? The only person missing from this movie scene was Kaylee.

"Yes," I replied to Erica. "That's Dr. Ellis' wife. Dad was cheating on mom with *her* too."

KJ then roared into action. "WHAT?"

"KJ, please go upstairs..."

"NO", he shot back. "I am *tired* of everyone telling me to go away. This is my family too, dammit!"

I had never heard KJ utter those words before. I wanted to calm him down, but then grandma yelled at the top of her lungs, "She has a GUN!" We all turned to see Dr. Ellis' wife point a gun directly at Officer Erica's head.

"Drop the gun, or else I will *blow* your brains out, right now!" Karen Ellis was serious.

Erica slowly put her gun on the floor and told us not to panic.

"Everything is going to be okay," she said directly to me and KJ. Is she kidding? We have a maniac about to kill my new sister I just discovered, and my boyfriend is standing here watching this.

"Where is your dad's medical bag?" asked Karen Ellis, getting angrier by the minute.

"Why do you need..." I started to ask, but wasn't allowed to finish.

"I need his cell phone!" replied Karen Ellie, before I was allowed to complete my thought.

"Oh, you mean the phone with all the nasty pictures and text messages between you and him?" I growled at her. "Oh, and the fact that your son isn't for Dr. Ellis, it's actually my dads?"

This made Karen Ellis laugh loudly. The gun was put under her arm, giving her two hands free to clap. "You are one smart girl," she said to me. "I never told your dad that my son was for him, how did you figure this out?"

"Because I'm smart, like you said," I sneered at her. "In reading all those text messages, I put two and two together."

Right then, Erica pushed Karen Ellis on the floor and the gun fell. They both wrestled for it, but Karen Ellis managed to get up and hit Erica with a chair she grabbed from the corner. While Erica lay motionless on the floor, Karen Ellis repointed the gun at her. Grandma couldn't take any of this. She jumped up and ran towards Karen Ellis with a big black and red umbrella in her hands, charging her like an angry bull. But Karen managed to turn and fired two shots at grandma, hitting her in both shoulders. We saw the umbrella drop to the ground as Grandma fell to the floor.

"Hey, go over and check on grandma," I whispered to Laurence. He ripped off his shirt and wrapped it around Grandma's shoulders to stop the pool of blood now rushing from her body. Karen Ellis now had her gun pointed back at Erica.

"All you had to do was mind your own business, but all you cops are the *same*!" she declared. "Always trying to play the hero. Well now, you're about to *die* like one!". She sounded more evil than any movie villain I had ever seen. We heard the gun *click* and then we heard two loud shots.

POW! POW!

Karen Ellis was the one who was hit, not Officer Erica. Who shot Karen Ellis in the back?

I looked over at the door and saw my little brother KJ. He picked up Erica's gun and delivered the fatal blow to Karen Ellis.

"KJ, give me the gun, please," I told my brother.

"Lex, I'm so sorry, she was going to *kill us*," he said. "I had to do it..."

"Hey, it's okay. I understand why you shot her." I tried to reassure him, but it wasn't working.

Erica pulled the gun from my hands and KJ immediately passed out beside me. I held him in my arms with my tears dropping onto his face. I just couldn't stop thinking how my little brother just killed one of my father's mistresses. You couldn't even write this in any screenplay. I had to be the only human being on this Planet who was going through all of this.

We saw Erica call for two ambulances, and then...

POW! Not again! Who keeps shooting? I thought Karen Ellis was...*dead!*

I stared beside me and Erica was now on the floor, motionless. I wasn't sure if she was dead. I turned and saw Laurence holding the gun in his hands.

Laurence shot Erica? But why?

"I'm sorry, Lexi, I never meant to hurt you. That's why I tried not to get close to you. After all, you...are my *sister*.

Wait. I was raped. I found out I have an older sister who is a cop. I just lost my father, my mother was nowhere to be found. My father's mistress just shot Grandma. My little brother just shot my father's mistress. And now...my boyfriend says he is my...*brother*? What's next? Will KJ turn out to be adopted? Will Kaylee end up being my sister? Will my mother flee the country and change her identity? I *dare* any movie studio to even consider this series of unfortunate events.

"Laurence, I'm confused. How can I be...your *sister*?" As long as I was falling down the bottomless pit of despair, I wanted to hear the answer.

"Karen and Dr. Ellis are my parents," he began to explain. "So, our little brother just killed *my mom*. Do you know what that means?"

"But wait," I stopped him. "I saw your mother when she picked you up. She looked nothing like Karen Ellis".

"Oh, her?" he said casually. "She was just a lady I paid to scoop me up".

I was utterly confused. "What?" I said to him with glazed eyes.

"Don't worry your pretty little head", he countered. "I'll make this easy for you. I'm going to kill *both* you and *our* little brother". His grin was evil and villainous, and I just wanted him gone. He pointed the gun directly at me, but almost two seconds after that, I heard the door burst open.

"Freeze! Hands up!" The police arrived just in time. They tackled Laurence to the ground and placed him in handcuffs. My heart dropped because I assumed I was going to die. While the cops walked Laurence outside, he turned towards me.

"Happy early birthday, sis. You have a *huge* surprise coming your way!" The evil smirk on his face added insult to a growing list of injuries that I was no longer able to bear. I knew whatever his "surprise" was, it was not going to be good.

Chapter 8

My Bitter/Sweet 16

I crawled over to Officer Erica to see if she was still alive. Another officer had rolled her over and onto her back. Erica took a deep frightening breath as if she had just gotten a mouth full of air. She ripped her shirt open and everyone there saw the bulletproof vest she was wearing. We all breathed a harmonious sigh of relief.

The paramedics gave Erica a quick check-up despite the presence of the bulletproof vest. Both KJ and I immediately ran to grandma, who was now laying on a stretcher in the ambulance.

"Grandma, everything will be okay," I assured her as I kissed her forehead. She started shaking uncontrollably. "What's wrong?" I asked the paramedic beside her.

"She's going into shock, she's lost a lot of blood," he explained. "Please back away so we can get her to the hospital."

I didn't know what to say. KJ looked as confused as I did and there was no way to comfort him.

And then, a bad situation kept getting worse.

Clink. My brother was in handcuffs.

"WHAT ARE YOU DOING?" I yelled to the officer who handcuffed KJ. "That's my little brother, what did he *do*?"

The tall officer did not respond to me. He glared at KJ while speaking. "Son, you are under arrest for the murder of Mrs. Karen Ellis!"

"Wait," I interjected. "She was going to kill us. He *saved our lives*, for crying out loud!"

No response from this tall maniac who obviously enjoyed his power. The words and the evil glare were still focused on my little brother.

"You have the right to remain silent. Anything you say can and *will be* used against you in a court of law. You have the right to an attorney. If you cannot afford one, then one will be appointed to you by the state..."

Okay, Robocop. Enough. He's a young kid who was protecting his family. Lay off!

I grabbed KJ and begged the crazy cop to let him go. But Robocop just kept pushing KJ out the door like a common criminal. I grabbed my crutches laying near the couch and hobbled outside on the front porch. I stared at all the police cars parked outside. What must the neighbors be thinking of us? Our little family did not deserve all this negative attention and I prayed for normal to come back. Then I heard my name.

"Alexis!" I know that voice. It could only be one person.

"Alexis!". Ms. Jackson. Ugh. The last person I wanted to hear right now was Ms. Jackson.

"What's going on over there, baby?" I didn't want to answer her. I turned my head back towards the car where KJ was sitting, handcuffed. I suddenly felt bad for ignoring Ms. Jackson. After all, she saved me from that horrible man who raped me. But the guilt trip was short-lived. There was too much going on for me to worry about nosy Ms. Jackson right now.

Erica ran to me after being checked out by the paramedics.

"Are you okay?" I asked.

"I'll be a little sore for a few days, but I'm fine."

"Erica, what are we going to do about KJ?" The whole world could see the frown on my face now.

"What? Where is he?" Erica was genuinely confused. She had not witnessed the brutal handcuffing of KJ. I pointed to the police car holding my brother hostage.

"Oh my God!" Erica turned redder than a beet. "Why the *hell* is he in that car?"

"They arrested him for killing Karen El... " I tried to explain. But Erica didn't need any more information. Before I finished my sentence, she ran to the officer who arrested KJ. All I could see were her arms swinging wildly back and forth as she yelled at the arresting officer. When she returned, she took three deep breaths before responding. "They're going to take him for questioning, they want to hear his side of the story. I *promise you* he's going to be alright. We both know this was a case of self-defense. Karen Ellis was going to kill me, and I'm sure she was going to kill you and KJ as well. I'll go with him just in case - to make sure they handle him properly."

After Erica left me, I felt both relieved and angry. I needed to be alone for a few minutes, so I walked back into the house and sat on the couch. I tried to empty all my thoughts and I found it easier to just stare at a new family photo we took just three weeks prior. I stared at my mom in the photo, then my dad. Then back to my mom. As I did this, I kept thinking, *Why is love so complicated? How can you love someone and then turn around and hurt them so badly?* My dad cheated on my mom - on multiple occasions - and it turned mom into a serial killer. I wish I had noticed mom's feelings before she found herself on the verge of a nervous breakdown. Why should children have to suffer like this? Parents are supposed to *protect* their kids, but instead my mother ended up killing the innocence right out of me. I was raped. Now my brother is going to jail for murder. Is this *love?*

I sat on that couch for a long time and stared at everything - the family photo, the television, even the ceiling. I didn't feel anything inside, I was running on empty. After a few more minutes, my eyes grew heavier and heavier and the room went dark.

Ring! Ring!

The phone jolted me out of my slumber. How long was I asleep? I could see the sunlight shining through the curtains. My mind was telling me I only slept for a few minutes, but my body told me it was much longer than that. I slowly wiped my eyes with my tired hands.

"Hello?" My voice was as tired as my hands. "Oh, Grandma, how are you doing?"

"Lex, the nurses and doctors here are taking really good care of me. I'm doing fine. I love you. Please give KJ a kiss for me."

I couldn't muster the strength to tell Grandma about KJ being arrested. She was already dealing with her own daughter being wanted for murder, as well as being shot by someone who claimed to be my fatgers second mistress and baby mother. Even a Lifetime movie doesn't get this twisted!

"I almost forgot, happy birthday, baby girl!" That's my Grandma - even with gunshots in her body, she never forgets to wish someone a happy birthday. In fact, with all that happened recently, even I forgot my own sweet 16th birthday. I can't think of any kid who willingly forgets their Sweet 16.

The birthday wish lifted my spirits momentarily. I ambled up the stairs with my crutches. I smelled really bad and decided on taking a shower. While looking for some proper shower attire, I noticed something sitting on the pink chest my parents bought me on my last birthday. It was my Sweet 16th birthday outfit. I couldn't believe it - when will I ever wear that and feel good about myself? I shook my head in disgust. My mind was already telling me the answer to my question. Since the pink outfit wasn't going anywhere, I chose more suitable attire and then headed to my much needed shower.

The water felt so good on my body, except for where I had been raped. There, I felt nothing but pain. After opening theshower door, I noticed a metal object on the floor. It was my mom's watch. I had no idea how it got there. I picked it up and looked at it for a few minutes. Images of my mom filled my head - I wondered where she was, and how she was doing. Then, without thinking, I see an inscription on the back of the watch. *HLP.*

Written in black marker. I had no clue what this meant - was it a name? A location? I racked my brain but the answer eluded me.

All that thinking made me hungry, so breakfast was my next mission. While hunting for food, I heard a knock on the door. I wasn't in the mood to talk to anyone. All I could think about was my little brother. How can I bring him home now?

Knock, knock.

I was even more angry that I was being interrupted while trying to find food. I opened the door.

"Erica, oh my God". She was not in uniform so I barely recognized her. I did notice how much cuter she appeared in normal clothes, compared to her police outfit.

"How are you feeling?" she asked.

"Honestly, I would be feeling *great* if you gave me good news about KJ", I replied.

"Well, KJ will be going in front of a judge today. I got him a lawyer. With some prayers and some good ol' finger crossing, he could be out on bail. Do you have any money laying around?"

"I do have access to my mom and dad's accounts," I told her.

"Good, because we may need about five hundred dollars..."

I sighed. If this will help KJ, then it's the best five hundred dollars I'll ever spend. I opened up my bank app on my phone and made the transfer to my account. But I realized I gave my debit card to my mom. Back to square one. I had to think fast. Oh yes, the emergency box!

My mom kept all her emergency stuff in a box in the kitchen closet. I found a credit card which had sufficient balance according to my life-saving phone app. In fact, I had almost three thousand dollars of instant spending power.

"What time does KJ appear before the judge?" I asked.

"At 11:00 am sharp", she answered.

"Darn, it's already 10:20, we have to rush". We were out the door within seconds.

We ran to the clerk's office after arriving at the courthouse. We were told KJ had already seen the judge due to another case being pushed back. We paid the bail but it seemed forever before he was released. I was relieved when KJ walked out to us.

"KJ, what the hell happened to you?" I asked. He had bruises all over his face in addition to a busted lip.

"They put me and Laurence in the same cell before they took him to the juvenile side. He jumped on me and started stomping on my face," explained KJ. "The cops pulled him off, but he told me he did it because I killed his mom. Then he spit on me."

I wanted to find Laurence and beat him until he couldn't move. How could he inflict this much pain on my little brother, when KJ was defending us from being killed? I could tell that Erica was equally upset about this event.

"Wait here, I'll be right back," she said, as she disappeared. A few minutes turned into an hour. I thought she was going to run away after seeing poor KJ in this condition.

"We can go now," she said as she appeared out of nowhere.

"What did you do, Erica?" I asked, not wanting to hear what she actually did.

"Nothing", she said calmly. "Everything is taken care of. Let's go."

Nobody was going to argue with this line of logic. She had a look in her eyes that could cut down the tallest tree. You don't mess with that look.

Erica was still shaking as she tried to open the car. I had to do something. I grabbed the keys out of her hand and opened the car. When we all got in, She quickly floored the pedal and raced off. Something was not right with her, but I dared not ask while she was in this state. We arrived at the hospital in one piece, although I felt as if I was going to die all over again in that speeding death trap. I noticed Dr. Ellis sitting on the steps leading up to the front door. I wondered if he knew about KJ killing his wife Karen.

"Stop, don't take another step!" warned Erica as she pointed her gun at Dr. Ellis.

"Wait, I only wanted to hug the kids and thank KJ for what he did," said a very nervous Dr. Ellis.

"What's going on now?" I asked Officer Erica. I saw way too many gunshots in the past few days. I didn't want to hear another gunshot for the rest of my life.

"Dr. Ellis, why do you want to thank KJ?" I asked. I wanted to be the first to ask this important question.

"Because KJ did me a favor!" replied the Doctor. "You see, Karen wanted my money and she threatened to kill me in my sleep. That's the reason I haven't been home in a while." We all stared at him, not believing what he had just said. "She found out I was in love with your dad, so she started blackmailing me. She threatened to tell your mom about us. We never meant to hurt you guys, but we were in *love!* We wanted to figure out how to tell everyone."

My nightmare of a life just got bigger and bigger. Let's add *gay dad* to this list.

"What?! You and my dad are in love?" asked a very confused KJ. "Two boys can't be in love with each other, can they?" I saw confusion all over my brother's face, and there was no room for any other emotion at this time. How does a young child process this kind of information?

"Yes, son, we were in love," said Dr. Ellis right back to this confused child.

"But why do you keep saying *we were* in love, like my dad is no longer around?"

That's when time stood still again. Being the horrible sister that I am, I forgot to tell KJ about dad passing away. I still couldn't believe that our father was...gone forever.

"KJ, come here," I gently said to my brother. "There's something you have to know."

I discreetly told KJ everything about dad and why mom was on the run. It was time for him to know everything. But KJ's little heart wasn't ready for this. He fell to the ground and cried the loudest cry I have ever heard from such a young body. We all could hear the pain in his cry now. It reminded me of the time I walked in on mom crying in the bathroom when I first witnessed her and dad arguing. I started to miss those days. I held my brother and tried to comfort him.

"KJ, I am here for you, okay?" said a comforting Officer Erica. "Please don't cry. I know you are hurting but you're going to get through this."

"Um, KJ, there *is* one more thing you need to know..." I debated whether to tell him, but he was already an emotional wreck, so one more piece of shocking news wouldn't hurt, right?

"KJ, Officer Erica here is actually...she is really...she's our older sister. There!"

KJ's eyes grew bigger than our china plates in our dining room break-front. "How..?"

I had to fill in the details for him. The same story that Officer Erica told me.

"So - if she's our sister, then why do you still call her Officer Erica?" he asked.

For someone who is emotionally wounded, this little brother still beats us on an intellectual level.

"Yea, I wonder the same thing," said Erica sarcastically. "You both can call me *Erica* from now on, deal?"

"Sure," I told her. We then went inside to see Grandma. Dr. Ellis smiled but gave a very strange look as he walked past us. I always considered him a very strange man. Nobody knew what would become of him, but at that moment, I didn't care.

We found Grandma and noticed she was eating her lunch. She was elated to see us.

"I am so happy to see you both. I just got off the phone with Grandpa." I knew Grandma didn't know Erica so I made all the proper introductions.

Grandma immediately felt comfortable with her. "I knew you were some-one special, the way you protected us last night," she told Erica.

I looked at everyone in this room. I had no idea what the future held for any of us. "What are we all going to do now? So much has happened. Does anyone have any idea?"

We all stared at each other for about five minutes. Finally, Grandma offered a solution.

"You and KJ can come and live with me and Grandpa in California. We have plenty of room for both of you."

"But what about their friends and their school?" asked Erica. "Why don't KJ and Lexi stay here with me?"

Grandma's face crinkled at the thought. How could Erica ask this when she was the new arrival in our lives? How could KJ and I trust someone we just met, even though she proved she can protect us.

"Erica, you can come and visit California anytime you want". Grandma was always negotiating.

"But KJ can't leave town until his actual court date, you know." A clever counteroffer from our newest sister. I was getting more impressed with Erica.

"Court date? For *what*?" asked Grandma. The mention of court made Grandma's blood boil.

"Well, KJ got in trouble for shooting Karen Ellis last night. But every-thing is going to be okay because this is a simple case of self-defense."

Grandma had to make one last negotiation - that was her style.

"Ok, I tell you what," she began. "I will stay here with all of you until all this nasty *court stuff* is over. Then I'll take all of you to California with me. How does that sound?"

Game over. Grandma always had the last word. Another lesson I learned - don't try to beat Grandma at her own game. She won this round.

"Erica," she continued, "would you help take care of us in the meantime?"

How could Erica refuse? She was dealing with the master negotiator. There was no other answer except "Of course."

This wonderful game was interrupted by my phone. It was the baker, Ms. Morgan.

"Hey, Alexis," she started. "I've been watching the news and ...well...I know your mom is not around...but...she did order a nice birthday cake for you. Do you want to come and..?"

I interrupted her. "No, I don't want it any more, I'm sorry." I just didn't feel like celebrating my Sweet 16 anymore.

"Hold on," said Erica, who grabbed the phone away from me. "Hello, this is Erica. I am on my way to pick up the birthday cake. Thanks."

"What are you doing?" I asked her in disbelief.

"Lex, you've been through SO much lately. You *deserve* to celebrate and I will make sure that you will have a good birthday!" Her voice and face were very determined and it was too late to stop this mission. We kissed Grandma goodbye and told her we would return later. After dropping us at home, Erica went on her mission to make my birthday unforgettable. But somehow, my Sweet 16 was already unforgettable, in a very bad way.

At this point, I started worrying about Kaylee. All calls went to voicemail. I hadn't heard from her since the day before. I wondered if something bad had happened to her. But just when I had that thought, she appeared at my front door.

"Kaylee, where have you been? I was looking for you and calling you all day," I said angrily.

"Well, when I dropped you at the building yesterday, the cops stopped me. I didn't want them to get suspicious of anything so I cussed them out. They arrested me and put me in a holding cell. That's where I spent the night."

I glared at her. My bestie spent the night in a jail cell? Just like my little brother? Was there anyone in my life who won't have something bad happen to them? She continued.

"My phone went dead - the only number I know by heart is my mom. I used the jail phone to call my mom so she could get me out." Then she paused. "Lex, I saw the blood all over the floor yesterday. What happened?"

I remembered I didn't get a chance to clean up all the blood she saw. I had to tell Kaylee everything, just like I told KJ almost everything. I told her about my rape. I told her about Laurence and Karen Ellis trying to kill us. Kaylee had a hard time processing this as well.

"Oh my gosh, Lex, girl, I am so sorry all this happened to you! Dang, man, so much craziness lately. You know you're my girl, right? You know I'm always here for you, right?"

"I know, girl. That's why I love you," I replied.

"Oh, and happy birthday, Lexi boo. Turn up, woot woot!"

"Girl, you sound so corny." I told her.

"Oh, whatever," she shot back.

Kaylee always made me feel safe and I needed someone to confide in just now. I hesitated and then I made my move.

"Kaylee, can I talk to you about something, girl to girl?"

"Girl, you know I'm here for you, I always have your back. What's on your mind?" she asked me.

With that, I opened the floodgates and talked more than I ever talked in my life.

"Kay, honestly, I don't know what to do anymore. My whole life has fallen apart, " I started slowly. I felt as if I had lost everyone in the world and it was hard to believe that Kaylee was still here. She hadn't changed - even though everything else had. What did that mean? Why was Kaylee the only constant in my life? *I shouldn't even think things like that - I don't want to jinx the one relationship I don't want to lose!* I decided to continue with no hesitation on my part.

"My whole life has fallen apart." I glanced towards the floor while saying this. "My mom is gone, my dad is gone *forever*, my virtue is gone." That last statement made me sigh even louder. "My brother may be going to jail, and that just leaves me. Truthfully, I just feel like I want to die." I didn't want to see Kaylee's reaction to this bizarre statement.

"I was trying to show my brave face, but inside I'm a total wreck. Today is my 16th birthday - it's supposed to be *sweet*, but it's not." I paused. "It's not, because my life is gone! I just want to die."

I waited for my best friend to say something, anything. I looked directly at her face while emphasizing my point. "I have no more peace inside of me. If I don't find peace soon, I feel like I'm going to kill myself." I had nothing more to say.

"Lexi, *PLEASE* don't ever talk like that," came the first set of long-awaited responses from Kaylee. "I don't know what I would do without you - you're the BEST thing in my life since my easy bake oven." She laughed while still maintaining the highest air of concern. "But seriously, you know that no matter what - we're in this together!"

There was nothing I could do except hug her and thank her for being the greatest and best friend anybody could ever ask for.

Kaylee said to me "Lexi, please don't ever talk like that. I don't know what i would do without you. You are the best thing that's happened to my life since my easy bake oven (She laughed), but seriously you know that no matter what, we're always in this together." I gave her a hug and truly thanked her for being the bestest best friend anybody could ever ask for. The topic then switched to something more lighter.

"So when is this party gonna start?" Kaylee was more excited about this party than I was now.

"Well ..." I started, "I don't want a party. I don't feel like celebrating --"

"Oh, what?" Kaylee raised her voice to the level of a scream. "You're having a party if it's the LAST thing I ever do!" I wish she didn't use those words. I wanted her around forever.

After that strict admonition, I saw my best friend dancing wildly on the floor. Someone should tell her how horrible a dancer she was, but I didn't care. My bestie can do whatever she wants, whenever she wants to.

"I'm going home to get ready for your festivities," said a very exhausted Kaylee after completing her semi-epileptic dance movements.

"Sure, but be back by 7 pm, ok?" I said.

"Don't worry, girl. I'll be here and I have a huge surprise for you," said Kaylee as she walked briskly out the door. I was definitely curious about this, but I didn't want to prompt her for too much information.

"It better be good --" I said to the back of her head.

"Trust me," she yelled back. "It's going to change your life forever."

Hmm, I thought. My life has already changed. Can Kaylee reverse everything that's happened so far? *That's* the only change I want right now. I started feeling a little better after Kaylee left. I knew nothing would be the same without my parents, but I was determined to make the most of it. I always showed strength through most of my life, but now the Universe was asking me to display superhuman strength. Nobody knows what they're capable of until they try. Right now, my only concern was the party.

I hopped upstairs to get ready, I wanted to look fly for the celebration. I pillaged through my closet looking for the outfit that screamed "fly" or "amazing". A knock interrupted my investigative search.

"Hi, Lexi, it's just us," yelled Erica and KJ. "Please don't come down until we call your name again."

I was excited - what could possibly be in store for me tonight, after all the horrific events that transpired? I freshened up and then I sat on my bed, in front of the mirror. I just stared at my reflection. Who was that looking back at me? That person certainly didn't look familiar. All I saw were cracks in my face, almost as if I had pieces of the original Lexi missing. But wait - there *were* pieces of me missing. I was slowly dissolving into nothing. I couldn't stand to look at the girl in the mirror. I needed to show the world a different Lexi, even if I had to rebuild her from scratch.

I put on an outfit that mom helped pick at the store. I wondered where she was now. She would be so proud to see me celebrating my Sweet 16. I really missed her. Something made me jump up and hobble over to my parents bedroom - I couldn't escape reminiscing about all the good times

I had with my parents. I noticed the matching outfit mom bought to wear at my party. I sat on my parents bed.

I thought about the last mother-daughter talk we had.

"Mom, when I turn 16, can I have sex?" I asked her.

"Baby, your private area is a beautiful, precious, valuable flower. You want to give it to someone who will be committed to you wholeheartedly - not just to someone who doesn't deserve you." She paused then looked directly into my eyes. The next words seemed to be a haunting premonition.

"The truth is, I can't be around you all day, everyday. I can't stop you if you want to have sex. But I want you to always keep my voice in your head. A voice that tells you to wait to give up that precious part of you." Yes, mom, I promise to always keep your voice in my head.

I wanted to honor my mom's words, and I was so ready for sex when I turned 16. But my beautiful, precious flower was stolen from me. If future sex is anything like that, I don't ever want to experience that again.

I was interrupted by another voice beside me.

"I miss them too, Lex." KJ was trying to reassure me. I didn't even hear him enter the room. "But I'm happy I have you. Now, please come downstairs. It's your birthday, so let's celebrate!"

KJ grabbed one crutch and we started to walk together. "You look cute, sis", he told me.

"Well, my little bro is growing up right in front of my eyes." I thought that would make him blush, but it didn't. We managed to make it to the bottom of the stairs and then --

"SURPRISE." The unanimous chorus came from many people. I was initially frightened and almost fell off the only two pieces of wood holding up my body. All my friends from school showed up, and I had mom to thank for that. She invited them all. I felt the tears flooding my face now.

"Erica, how did you get everyone here?" Erica could see the shock cemented on my face.

"That's all KJ," she said. "While I shopped, KJ called everyone."

I looked at KJ. He was growing so fast and showing so much respon-sibility now.

"Erica, I don't know --"

"Girl, please." Erica was almost annoyed that I was thanking her. "You have a big sister now who cares so much for you. I got you, girl." The smile on my face was sufficient for her. I moved around slowly to address each friend who showed up.I noticed the room was clean - no blood, no mess. I was relieved.

I scoured the room for familiar faces - but I didn't see Kaylee. Her phone was still going to voicemail like before. Hopefully she was on her way. I know she is not going to let me down on the biggest night of my life. I wanted to enjoy myself so I made crude attempts at dancing.

Thirty minutes later and still no Kaylee. Now I was starting to worry. People were getting tired and I wanted her to show up before everyone left. I heard the first few words of "Happy Birthday to you..." Then Erica's face suddenly cringed.

"Lexi, turn on the news. Hurry!" The urgency hit me like a ton of bricks.

I couldn't believe what I was hearing and seeing - Laurence had been released from jail and he was out on bail. He pushed his father - Dr. Ellie - from the top of the hospital building. I saw the cops put him into the squad car and then I heard him say these chilling words - to me.

"Alexis Samuels, this is ALL on you! His blood is on YOUR hands."

My body froze. I couldn't move the crutches if my life depended on it. I felt everyone stare at me now. How could Laurence ruin my Sweet 16 celebration. If I could be any animal now, I wish I was a turtle - so I could retreat into my shell. I looked around the room. Everyone started to leave, their heads shaking. I had no idea what to say to them. I couldn't speak, I couldn't move. I slowly sat on the couch, and Erica and KJ joined me in complete silence.

After a long time, Erica spoke first. "Lex, you know that wasn't really your fault, right?"

I just stared at her without responding. In my mind, I knew one thing and one thing only - this chaos would never end. It was meant to happen, and it was meant to get worse. *Happy Sweet 16th birthday to me.*

Chapter 9

"Kenton Samuels, A Celebration Of Life"

Through all the pain, hurt, and anger I was feeling, I still had to plan my dad's funeral. My grandma was released from the hospital, but she couldn't do much because of what she endured from her gunshot wounds. She did assure me she would do whatever she could to help me with the funeral arrangements.

I was worried because I never heard back from Kaylee. I tried calling her house - still no answer. I decided I would drive by and check on her - it wasn't like her to say she was going to be at my party and then not show up. I started thinking the worst, it seemed to be my new normal.

I wanted my dad's funeral to be a celebration of his life. Even though the last week of his life was turned upside down, I wanted everyone to remember the good that he did while he was on this earth. I even asked grandma about this, and she told me I was a very wise person. "Are you sure you just turned only 16?" was the question she asked me. I needed a ride to the funeral home.

"Erica, can you take me to the funeral home?" I asked her over the phone. "The church doesn't want anything to do with us because of everything they saw on the news."

"Sure, I'll be there as soon as I finish my rounds," she told me.

I started hopping upstairs to retrieve my coat when my phone started to vibrate obnoxiously. I glanced at the screen. *Monarchy Juvenile Correctional Facility.* Who could that be, I wondered? I clicked the button. "Uh, hello?" I said very discreetly.

"Hello, is this Alexis Samuels?" said a strong male voice on the other end.

"Yes, may I ask who's calling?" I wanted to be polite but I was more annoyed at this interruption.

"Yes, this is Warden Johnathan Brown. I was calling because we have an inmate here by the name of Laurence E. Bowers. Are you familiar with that name?"

Unfortunately, I was.

"Yes, sir I am," I continued. "What's going on, I don't have a lot of time --"

"Well," said Mr. Brown unapologetically, "Mr. Bowers got into a fight and he killed two 15-year old boys before dying from stab wounds to the face and body." He paused, waiting for my reaction. "I'm calling you because he named you as a person of contact."

The chaos I had feared had shown up even bigger and stronger now. If chaos was an animal, it would be Tyrannosaurus Rex.

"Um, sir," I was in no mood for this, "I don't know why he would list me as a contact. He is actually an enemy of this family." I was hoping that would be the end.

It wasn't. "Is that right?" continued the robotic Warden. "I'm so sorry to hear this. I have his belongings here - if you want to come and pick them up, I'd be happy to release them to you."

I thought before responding. "I am not interested in any of Laurence's belongings right now. Goodbye, sir."

The phone went dead. I didn't care about being polite. Laurence was gone. Why would I want something to remind me of *him*? I had to sit down for a few seconds. I couldn't hold back the tears. I cried harder than I ever have in my life this past week. I was just starting to forget about Laurence and that Warden had to throw a cruel reminder in my face.

"Hey, what's wrong now?" Erica just walked in and sat right beside me.

"You won't believe what I just heard." I described the whole situation to her.

"Girl, no. He *didn't*." She smacked the stairs with her open palm when she heard this. "Well, let's forget Laurence. You have more important things to worry about now."

As we left the house, we noticed Grandma sleeping soundly on the couch. Thank goodness she would be home when KJ got in from school. As we drove away, I thought I saw Kaylees car parked on the side of the road, near the entrance to our house. Maybe I'm hallucinating...maybe I missed her so much that *everything* reminded me of her. I decided not to focus on this now.

We pulled up to the funeral home but Erica looked concerned.

"Lexi, there's something I have to tell you ..." she said as her gaze was directed to the road in front of her. "I have to get something off my chest - right now."

My mind started going through all the possible options now. Did something happen to Kaylee? Was Erica in trouble now?

"I'm the one that got Laurence killed --" she said.

"Oh, my God. Why? How??" I shot back. I was angry she was telling me this.

"Well, he beat up KJ. And then he blamed you for his father's death. That was the last straw!" She still didn't look at me. "I dated one of the officers at the correctional facility, briefly. That officer paid two guys to rough him up. But I didn't know that they would KILL him..."

How much crap can fit inside a 16-year olds brain? I was scared there was no more room left inside me.

"WOW, Erica. Not you, too!" I screamed at her.

"What do you mean, 'not me, too'? She asked.

"I mean, you know all the stuff I've been going through lately. And now you go and do - *this?*" I didn't even know what name to give it.

"Lexi, I told you before. Now that I'm in your life - and KJ's life - you both will have nothing to worry about. I *meant* those words. I didn't mean for him to die. I just wanted to scare him, that's all."

I looked at her in pure disgust and then I ran out of the car. Erica tried to catch up to me. If it wasn't for these evil crutches, she would never have caught with me.

"Lexi, please wait," she pleaded. "I'm sorry, I was just protecting you and KJ."

"Protect us from *what*, Erica? He was locked up, and we were safe!" How could she not understand that as an officer of the law?

"But that's just it," she tried to explain. "They were playing the insanity card. He would've been out eventually, so I wanted to scare him. Just enough so he wouldn't even think about bothering you guys again..."

What could I possibly say to this? Did she expect me to just say *Thank you for killing Laurence and protecting us*? I continued staring at her. She continued her weak explanation.

"You have lost so much lately, but I just found both of you. I was NOT going to lose you." She stopped and looked away. "I did what I did because I care about you both."

I didn't know whether to be mad or grateful to her now. At least she cared enough about me and KJ to do *something* to protect us. Maybe it wasn't the best reaction, but it was something.

"Please forgive me, Lexi". She was on the brink of tears.

"I forgive you, Erica". I walked closer to her. "But, if you ever feel like protecting us in the future, then *please* consult with us before doing something crazy!"

"I got you, sis. I promise." End of discussion.

We went inside and spoke to Mr. Rob, the funeral director.

"Here's all the packages we have". He shoved a giant book in front of us and we were immediately confused with the selections. I was even impressed how people were willing to go to financial extremes to bury their loved ones.

"I can help your confusion." He had noticed the pained look on both of our faces. "Your mom and dad already made arrangements for themselves. The only thing they didn't choose was the Hearse and the flower colors."

"Hmm," I started. "That's an easy decision. Thanks for that information."

Colors - what would dad have liked. He was always partial to black and yellow. So I picked the gold rose royce to carry his coffin and Black and yellow flowers. After all, dad deserved the colors of royalty, and those colors are as close as we can get to royalty.

"Very good", said a happy Mr. Rob. It was unusual to see such a happy face in a funeral parlor. "One more question - what day would you select for this event?"

I glanced at Erica for an answer.

"Well, he's your dad also, so you choose the date," I reminded her. She was obviously impressed with this decision.

"Really, Lexi?" She almost blushed. "That means a lot to me, sis."

Erica pondered this and then looked directly at Mr. Rob.

"How soon can you have everything ready?"

"My team and I can have everything arranged today." Mr. Rob truly enjoyed his profession.

"Perfect. I know it's soon, but I think we should do this tomorrow," said a less enthusiastic Erica. "The sooner we begin, the faster the healing process can start."

Where did that answer come from? I didn't believe for one second there would even be any more healing moments in my twisted life. Now it was the funeral director's turn for confusion.

"Are you sure that's enough time to gather your loved ones?" Mr. Rob stepped in front of both of us and we could smell the cheap gel on his thinning hair.

"Excuse me, Mr. Rob," I intervened. "I'd have to agree with my sister here". I made a deliberate effort to point at Erica. "We really don't have anyone coming from out of town. My dad's mother is in Jamaica with my aunts and uncles. But --" A thought just flashed in my head. "If you have WiFi here, we can have a video service so they can be part of my dad's home going celebration."

Mr. Rob scratched his chin and reflected for a minute. "Yes, we can absolutely do that for you. Well, ladies, the service will start tomorrow at 3 PM if that's acceptable to you."

The time was acceptable. "Okay, we will see you all in the morning. I'll send a limo to your house around 2 PM to bring you here."

Erica and I were pleased at this last minute accommodation. We turned towards the door and then Mr. Rob threw one final question, as if his whole life revolved around questions. His eyes seemed a little beadier somehow, but we didn't want to waste time assessing his hasty change of personality. "Excuse me, but do you both want to have a viewing first?". Ah, yes, the public viewing. Every funeral has those, right? I didn't know, and I really didn't care.

"No, but it's okay to have an open casket," I said. "I hope that answers all your questions, sir." I had had enough of Mr. Rob, who eagerly agreed with my final suggestion.

"Can you believe that man?" I asked Erica. I was glad I wasn't related to him somehow.

"Never mind him", said Erica. "He's a strange bird, but he's just doing his miserable job."

"I guess". I muttered. I hated funeral homes and I didn't want to plan any more funerals if I could help it. "Hey, can we swing by Kaylee's house to make sure she's ok?" I quickly checked Erica's face for any sign of approval. "Sure" - there was my sign of approval.

We approached Kaylee's house from a direction I hardly used, and we noticed dozens of police and paramedics surrounding the house. There was even someone from the - wait - *coroner's office*? I was going to pray that God would have pity on me and command the world to just stop for a few seconds, but I knew that prayer would be in vain.

"Oh God, NO. Please, PLEASE tell me this isn't happening - PLEASE!" I was now begging God to be nice to me just this one time. I never begged God for anything before.

"Lexi, stay in the car, I'll find out what's going on. Don't move!" Erica was now in charge and nobody would dare disrespect her. She had the power of the badge behind her name. I stared out the window as Erica gathered information. Then I noticed Erica's hand grabbing her mouth and never leaving it. This was no accident. That gesture meant that "bad" just went to "worse".

"Lexi, please don't panic --" said Erica upon re-entering the car.

I started to panic. How can any person not panic when the Coroner was in front of the house?

"Erica...just...tell...me...please..." My voice was quivering.

"Ok, when Kaylee's mom didn't show up to work this morning, her coworker Helen called the police". Erica's voice was shaking also. "The police went to check and when they arrived here, they saw blood on the front door..."

I didn't want to hear anymore. "Oh my God, no..." That statement came out of nowhere.

"The police burst the door open and found Kaylee's mom laying on the floor. Dead. Covered in blood - with a hammer laying next to her."

Stop talking, Erica. Please don't say another word.

"Then they found Kaylee's father". Erica ignored my wishes and simply continued on. "He was in the bathtub with multiple stab wounds. "But how? They are divorced. What was he even doing there"?, I interjected. I don't know Lexi but that's not all. Kaylee's sister was laying in her bed. She had been smothered to death."

It was not enough that I had to lose my family, one by one. Now in a twisted turn of events, the devil wanted to inflict the same pain on my best friend.

"STOP!" The one word that causes all time to freeze. I had to utter it now. "OH MY GOD," I added for extra effect. I covered my mouth with my Sweet 16 hands, which should have been still at the party, celebrating.

"Where is Kaylee, then?" I suddenly remembered that Kaylee may still be alive.

"Um, they said there was a struggle of some kind. They believe whoever did this might have taken Kaylee..."

Might have taken Kaylee? Where? Who would want Kaylee like this?

Erica saw the desperation rising inside of me, like a tidal wave. The wave was about to wipe out an entire town. She knew I reached my limit - this was Kaylee we were talking about. The one constant in my life. And now, that constant is gone? Without her, who do I have left?

"Wait," I told Erica. "Something doesn't add up. Let's go home. I just remembered something."

As we approached the house, we turned a corner where I thought I had seen Kaylee's car earlier.

"Stop". Erica was confused. I didn't have time to explain. I exited the car and walked up to the car I saw earlier. Yes! It *was* Kaylee's car. I noticed the cell phone on the front seat and her keys were still in the ignition!

"I knew it," I told Erica. "That's Kaylee's car, right there!"

We both ran into the house. Grandma was finally awake.

"Grandma, have you seen Kaylee?" I asked. No, she didn't. My mind was racing now. I recalled Laurence telling me about a "huge surprise". Was this his idea of a sick joke? Did he have something to do with this? Just then, Erica hung up her cell phone. "Lexi, that was my captain. He said they found Kaylee's shoes and a piece of her shirt. They both had blood on them." She paused. "That's a sign she may still be alive."

"Ok, but if they had blood on them, how is she still alive?" I wanted to get used to expecting the worst with every situation.

"Because," Erica said quickly before I accepted the worst case, "they think she may be just simply hurt real bad, and not dead."

Grandma didn't say a word. She just absorbed all this information. She seemed to be the type of person who couldn't come to a conclusion without data.

"Everyone, please hold hands. It's time to pray and reach out for help." That's the only thing I didn't consider - prayer. I was looking for someone on this earth to help me process what was happening, and I felt ashamed I had given up on the one person who already had all the answers.

Grandma prayed first. Erica followed, but she struggled. She didn't know how to pray. Then Grandma offered the greatest advice, "Pray what's in your heart. God already knows your heart."

KJ was next. I was last in line. I already knew what to say.

"God, who sits high and looks low, who has created all things living and beautiful, we need you now. We come to you on behalf of everything that's been happening in my life and in our family's lives. You can see we are struggling to keep our heads above water. Everywhere we turn, bad things surround us. We come to you, asking in faith, that you bring Kaylee home to us. We ask that you reveal the people behind her family's death, if that be your will. Comfort us and keep us near the right path. You have ordered our steps already. Please be with us tomorrow at the funeral. We turn my father over to you, now. We pray all this in your loving and humble name. Amen."

Somehow I knew the words would come. I wasn't trying to impress anyone. I was trying to make sure God heard me that evening. Even if I didn't get the answer I needed, God knew what was in my heart. My prayer was followed by a chorus of "Amens".

"Do you need me to stay with you tonight?" asked Erica.

"Yes," I replied, without thinking. "We could use the comfort." In truth, I was the only one needing comforting that night. Erica went home to gather her clothes for the funeral. I left KJ and Grandma on the couch, while I laid on my bed upstairs. I gazed at the ceiling while I wiggled my good leg back and forth. My body had an unlimited amount of tears in reserve and my eyes had no trouble letting them flow. The tears put me to sleep. I remember waking up in the night screaming, causing Erica to rush to my side.

"I must have had a nightmare," I told her. She gave me a reassuring pat on the back with the standard "everything will be okay" speech. Why do people insist on saying that when *they* know everything will not be okay? I promised myself never to believe anyone when they said that. Erica decided to lay close to me. I needed someone close. I woke up a few hours later and found Erica nowhere in sight. I let my body enter panic mode when Erica suddenly appeared.

"Where were you?" I asked in anger.

"I was getting dressed. We have to go soon, you have to get ready now."

"Ok". I wanted to check my phone first to see if Kaylee called or texted. Nothing. I quickly checked all my social media accounts, but they grimly reminded me that Kaylee was offline for more than 48 hours now.

I remember my prayer to God. I looked up to the ceiling and told God "I'm keeping the faith on this one." I did remember an old Bible verse that said "Ask and ye shall receive". Why would the Bible lie about that? I jumped in the shower to get ready. I noticed the pain *down there* had subsided. Hopefully the pain in my soul would leave also.

"Lexi, hurry up." KJ was now rushing me. The Limo was outside waiting for us.I hurried downstairs as fast as I possibly could to my surprise, there was my family nicely cleaned up and dressed to kill.

"We need a picture of this," said a very sentimental Grandma who jumped right into action. "Smile guys" she happily uttered. After about four different poses, we finally swooped into the waiting Limo. This was my first time in a Limo and I wish it happened under better circumstances but I couldn't stay inside of my head for too long. As we rolled up to the funeral home, We didn't see many people outside or inside for that matter. I was surprised to see my dad's colleagues sitting in the pews.

We walked somberly down the aisle, toward a black casket with wood grain trimmings and brass bars around it. I stayed at the casket while others marched by in slow procession. Dad looked so peaceful at rest. I was really going to miss him. We discovered that both mom and dad selected a nice package from Mr. Rob, the funeral director. I feared the service would be too long, but it was just right. We all stood at the podium and gave miniq eulogies, even Erica. I was surprised to see her up there, but I would have regretted it if she didn't.

We all headed home after the service. Erica ordered food for the guests who wanted to stop by. After a few minutes, the guests started trickling in. The first guest was Pastor Clarke, who we referred to as just PC.

"Alexis, my girl, you did a good job today. Your parents would be very proud of you. You took control and got things done." PC was trying to be supportive in our time of need. "You're a very strong, young lady. We are all proud of you."

"Thank you, PC," I said.

"And just know," he continued, "we are praying for you and your family. Our doors are always open to you."

My angelic face went demon red at that statement. *Our doors are always open to you? Really?*

My anger took over. "But your doors weren't open for my dad when we asked to have his funeral there, right?" Erica could see the steam coming out of my ears. She tried to intervene, but I jerked my shoulder away from her and fell to the ground.

"Don't touch me," I commanded her. I was done with everybody and everything.

"Everyone, get out!" I yelled to all the guests. My voice grew louder in intensity. "OUT"

Grandma was now awakened like a bear out of hibernation. "Lexi, what are you doing --"

"Grandma," I interrupted before she could lay down the law, "I do NOT want to hear it. Leave me alone, I want to be by myself."

"Fine." Grandma knew when I needed to be alone. "Erica, can you take me to the pharmacy to get my medication? KJ, you stay here with Lexi." Even when Grandma wasn't in charge, she was always in charge. I got tired of the atmosphere downstairs, so I headed for more safer spaces. "KJ, please fold the tables back up and take them to the shed out back." I had to show him who was in charge now. I retreated to my safe space upstairs. Here, nobody could tell me what to do.

Three minutes of solitude passed. Then I heard music. It was the loudest, strangest music I had ever heard. Who would play music this loud at this time of day? I grabbed my crutches to investigate. So much for personal solitude and for being in charge.

Chapter 10

"DEVASTATED GRIEVANCE"

I had just arrived home after the funeral service. I found out my best friend's family had been murdered and my best friend is missing. I didn't have the strength to hear any more bad news. I prayed to God again, while heading down stairs. *God, please protect us. Please don't let this be another intruder doing bad things.*

It wasn't an intruder. I saw KJ sitting on the couch, kissing some random girl - or maybe his girlfriend?

"KJ". I called his name, no answer. I tried two more times. No answer. I felt the anger rise within me again. The kissing continued without interruption. This had to stop. I picked up a crutch and threw it in his direction. No response. *My God, how can I get them to stop?* I had an idea. I grabbed a spray bottle filled with water that mom used to water her plants with. Perfect. Water was flying everywhere and landed perfectly on their faces.

"STUPID! Why did you do that?" KJ was angrier than a hungry Doberman.

I was just about to answer, then changed my response. "Did you just call me - 'stupid'?" I asked while squinting my eyes like Clint Eastwood in one of those western movies, yeah I'm an old soul..

"I sure did!," he responded. "Because you sprayed us with water."

"I wouldn't have sprayed you if you had heard me call your name three times, or have your tongue inside this little girl's mouth!" Someone had to play the Parent in this room, and I grabbed this role with delight.

"Who are you calling a little girl?" said the little girl whose tongue was just attacked by my brother's mouth. "I have a name - it's *Jasmine*". Then she started walking away from both me and KJ. "Oh and FYI", she said in her I'm-a-big-girl-voice, "I am more woman than you could EVER be!" Unbelievable. Dad must be turning over in his grave now.

"KJ, what makes you think that *that* was okay? How can you do that right after we buried daddy? You should be sad and grieving, like me."

KJ stared at me for five seconds, then shook his head.

"What's with the head shake?" I was genuinely curious.

"Lexi, I'm trying really hard not to hurt your feelings." I didn't understand what KJ meant by this.

"What do you mean, 'you don't want to hurt my feelings'," I parroted back to him, almost mocking him.

"Lexi, you've been acting like you're all grown up, but then you cry all over the place." I maintained my look of confusion.

"Yes, that's right. I know you've been crying because Erica told me when we went to the store to buy your birthday stuff --"

"KJ, you really don't know what you're talking about here. Please be quiet!" The Parent inside of me wanted to spank him now.

"So, I have to be quiet because I just struck a nerve?" KJ was becoming the master at knowing how to hit people's buttons. When he was young, he was a simple brat. Now, he was showing off his Ph.D in Brat. I had to nip this in the bud.

"No", my voice grew dimmer, "you should be quiet because you have no idea what I've been going through." Maybe those words would calm him down and put some empathy in him.

"Aww, boohoo! You're always playing the victim and wanting attention." I was wrong, nothing would produce empathy in his brat body.

"KJ, where is this attitude coming from?" I was scared to see the person he was growing into.

"Lexi, I was getting tired of mom and dad always paying more attention to you than to me." Ok, now we're getting somewhere.

"KJ, don't say that, it's just not true." I was hoping this really wasn't true.

"YES! Yes, it is true. Have you ever wondered why I stay in my room all day playing my games?" I did wonder about that, actually. "Because I always felt like I'm in the way. I'm the third wheel."

I digested everything KJ was saying, whether I believed it or now. I had to manage this conversation, before it got way out of hand.

"But, KJ, listen to me. Dad spent a lot of time with you, right? He went to all of your games, didn't he?" The angry Parent in me was fast becoming the nurturing Parent.

"Yes, you're right," he admitted. "Dad went to all of my games, but while I was out there on the field, I would look up and see dad laughing and flirting with some of the mothers in the stands. That was his excuse to get away from mom, so he could have freedom to flirt." I couldn't believe KJ actually saw this and didn't say anything before.

"So why didn't you say anything?" My inner voice matched my outer voice perfectly that time.

"Because..." his eyes darted away from me, "daddy told me not to say anything." He said it was a father-son code. Anyway, I'm not a snitch like you." He folded his arms and hung his head.

I found myself blindly looking for footing in a sea of new emotions. My little brother was blowing me away because I didn't expect this type of energy from him. "Dang, bro". I was trying hard to be emotionally self-aware. "All this, because I sprayed you with a little water?"

"No", he said. "Actually, I've been wanting to say this to you for the longest time. This was just the right time to say it, because I'm so - I'm so mad at you!" He paused while his mind searched for the right words to follow. "You treat me like a little kid, but I understand more stuff than you give me credit for. When are you going to see that?"

I had to think. Did I always do that? I always thought I could read KJ, but lately I can't even read myself.

"So, what do you want from me --" I didn't know what to say, really.

"For starters, tell me stuff when it happens, not when it's already out of control."

"Fine". I hated this conversation. "What else?" I wanted this to end.

"Treat me with respect. I know I'm your little brother, but I have feelings too, you know." Oh, I knew. But at that moment, I wanted to ask God why I wasn't an only child.

"Ok, I get that." I conceded, hoping this was his last request. "Treat you with respect. What else?" I was checking off his demands like a hostage negotiator.

"Yeah. If anybody ever does something to you again, tell me so I can *kick their asses!*" There's the tiger I always wanted to see. "Stop cursing," was my reply to the boy growing into a man right in front of me. "But, ok. I got you, bro. You'll be the first to know."

Now that I survived that drama, my attention turned to the other female in the room.

"KJ, how did Jasmine get here so fast anyway?"

"Um, she was in the backyard waiting for me. That's why I didn't go with Erica and Grandma." I could either slap him or high-five him for this response. But I nodded my head in approval. I was actually proud of him. "Boy, you are one slick dude, huh?"

"Hey, I learn from my big sister." Yes, you do. Don't ever forget that.

My phone suddenly interrupted this perfectly made-for-tv moment.

"Lexi" - it was Grandma - "are you sitting down?" I froze. No good news ever comes to those who are seated.

"Grandma, actually I'm --"

"Sit down, baby." The three words I hated the most in this world.

"I'm sitting". Grandma heard my sigh from wherever she was. I think the whole world heard me sigh just then.

"Lex, I bought a candle to bring to Kaylee's house. I put it in front of the house to honor her and her family." Nice gesture, Grandma, but where's the bad news I'm expecting. Remember the part about people who sit?

"Erica and I saw lots of people there, crying and comforting each other. Kaylee's cousins were there and someone told them..." She stopped. I heard the emotion in her voice, far away.

"Someone told them they found the body of a teenage girl - she was wearing the same shirt and shoes Kaylee had on when she disappeared ..." More strained silence. I already knew the ending to this story.

"Lex, the body was found burned - near a tree - three miles from Kaylee's house. The police...the police believe it's...Kaylee... they're looking at dental --" The phone went dead. Not because of bad weather. Because I threw my phone hard on the floor. Because I never wanted that phone to serve as a bearer of bad news. Ever. My only friend in the world was gone. My mom was gone. My dad was gone. My friend who almost became my boyfriend was gone. Was I really sure that Grandma and KJ were really here, or were they figments of my imagination?

Losing a friend is hard. But losing a best friend who was really a mirrored reflection of yourself is incomprehensible. There are friends who bring you chocolate and cuss out your enemies. They should be treasured. But Kaylee was one in a billion. She was the friend who would show up at your house with a shovel, a rug, and ask no questions. She would do anything for me. I had the chance to make her stay when she showed up at my house. Why didn't I do that? She would still be alive today.

The guilt was killing me. I was responsible for Kaylee's death.

Now sadness became anger. And anger was slowly turning into vengeance. Who would be that cruel that they would kill and burn Kaylee, then kill her whole family? I slapped my face hard to make sure this was real. But reality is a harsh teacher ready to punish. I yelled to God "Please find Kaylee." But God had other plans. My best friend was gone. Everybody I loved was vanishing before my eyes.

"Lexi, what's wrong?" KJ hadn't heard the news.

"Jr, I don't know how to tell you this..." He did say he wanted me to start hearing the truth, didn't he? "

"Jr. they found Kaylee..." His eyes lit up.

"That's good. Where is she?" The truth, Lexi, the truth...

"NO! You don't understand!" Go easy, he doesn't know the truth yet. "They found her *body*, *burned*. A few miles from her house. She's...she's gone...forever...she ..." My mouth refused to say "that" word. But KJ understood. His body understood and his mind understood.

"NOOOOOOO," he cried so hard. His lungs almost burst. "WHY? WHY? WHY?? ... It was as if he had lost his best friend also. The floor was full of our tears and we waded through that as we climbed upstairs. Then we heard the door open.

"Lexi". Grandma and Erica rushed inside the house. Erica followed me and KJ while Grandma hugged the bottom of the rails.

"Erica..." I fell into her arms as she provided a warm enclosure for both me and KJ. Part of me wanted to stay embraced and part of me wanted to escape. I felt both parts fight each other, and eventually the part of me that wanted out was victorious. I broke free like a wild horse and escaped to my room.

I opened the drawer on my nightstand. There were so many pictures of places that me and Kaylee visited. There was me and Kaylee on a school trip to D.C. That's when we found out Kaylee was allergic to seafood. The girl blew up like a puffer fish, and that picture was evidence of that. The more pictures I viewed, the more emotional I became. I had enough. I returned them back to hiding in the drawer where they couldn't bother anyone, anymore. Then I started thinking of all the people in my life - the people I would never see again.

Kaylee. Mom. Dad. Dr. Ellis. Karen Ellis. Laurence. Kaylee's family. All those innocent people my mom killed. Could I have prevented any of this?

But who was left? What about KJ? Who would be there for him when he gets older and starts wondering about all of this. I immediately removed myself from consideration. I'm no savior. I couldn't even save my own parent's marriage, or their lives. And then it hit me.

KJ would be better off without me.

I made my decision. In my parent's room was a bottle of oxy from when my dad threw his back out. I poured half the bottle into my willing hands and then swallowed them with the help of a bottle of water I found by the door. I did not hesitate. It was time. I sat on the edge of my parent's bed and stared fondly at a picture of them sitting on the dresser. What a great picture. They looked so happy and in love. That picture is so ...wait...I see four people in that picture...oh now there's more? Maybe if I --

The room went dark.

When my eyes finally opened, I was being wheeled on a stretcher and rushed down a pristine hall with thick tubes protruding from my mouth. I was surrounded by a team of people all harmoniously panicking and moving in the same direction. I was having an out-of-body experience. My eyes followed the nurses and doctors, dressed in white, as they pushed me down the hall like a speeding bullet train. They pushed open a door labeled OR 21. My eyes saw everything - how they pumped my stomach, how they monitored my blood pressure and vitals. I couldn't stop looking. Then the head doctor went back into the hall. My eyes followed him to the waiting area.

"Excuse me, are you the family of Alexis Samuels?" he asked my family. KJ, Grandma and Erica were all there, pacing new groove lines into the just-cleaned hospital floor.

"Alexis is in the OR now, but her kidney and liver functions are low. She swallowed half a bottle of pills.. Some had dissolved, but we were able to pump out about 37 pills from her stomach."

"Doctor, will she be okay? Will she live?" Grandma wanted me alive at all costs.

"Well, ma'am", he said to her, "I'm not sure of anything now. I can only tell you that the next 24 hours are crucial. If you folks believe in prayer, now's the time to pray. In the meantime, I have to call the social worker from the Division of Children and Family Services --"

"Excuse me, why?" Grandma would not have any of this. She wanted her baby home.

"Ma'am", said a doctor trying to be calm, "When a child comes in because of an attempted suicide, we have to notify the Division of Children and Family Services. I'm sorry, but that's our protocol.

It was Erica's turn to intervene. "Doctor, thank you. I'm a police officer, and that's my little sister you're treating in there. I know the protocol, but *believe me* when I say - that girl that you have laying in there - is truly loved by us. Please do everything you can to save her life. We have lost a LOT this week!" The doctor would never know just how much we had lost, so why even tell him? "Lexi has lost a lot - her parents, her best friend - all in the same week!!" They were all checking for the doctor's reaction to this emotional outburst. Nothing, no emotion. Do they train doctors to lose all emotions once they graduate medical school?

The Doctor looked at KJ, then Grandma, then Erica. His hands still didn't know what to do.

"I understand, Officer" he said in a gentle tone infused with the smallest emotion he could muster. "I promise we will do everything we can for her."

"Thank you, doctor". Erica wanted to have the last word but knew empty words when she heard them.

My hovering eyes were taking all this in. I suddenly felt stupid for attempting to take my own life. In that moment I actually witnessed the depth of my family's love for me and how much they'd miss me if I'd left them. How could I ever make this up to them? I began to float back to the room where they had my body. I sat on the side of the bed. I couldn't even look at myself - my broken body with tubes coming out of - everywhere. I laid whatever form I had on that bed. Even spirits need to rest.

"Baby girl, what have you done?"

I looked up and it was - *dad*? Wait, was I alive or dead? I turned and saw my body, still lifeless in the hospital room. What was happening? I looked directly into my father's eyes.

"You're going to be okay". His words were so comforting, so soothing. I wanted to hear him talk forever. "It's not your time, yet. You have to be there for KJ. He needs you now."

I continued staring at him. Was he an angel, or a nightmare? Did I hallucinate his death? Were the pills making me hallucinate now?

"Before I go, I only ask that you forgive me. I want you to keep your eyes open, ok? Now go back into your body ..." His spirit disappeared. The voice was gone. My eyes were opened.

I was looking directly into their faces now. Grandma, Erica, and KJ. They all surrounded my hospital bed. I was groggy and in so much pain. I wondered how long I was laying there. I wanted to see dad again. But one thing was certain - I was happy to be alive. Even if that meant posing as normal in the wake of all my recent losses.

Chapter 11

"THE ULTIMATE BETRAYAL & THE REALITY"

After waking up in the hospital, I stayed there for a few more days, until I was finally released. I thought Erica and Grandma were taking me home, but then I was told the social worker would be taking me home because they had errands to run.

"Hey, KJ can't wait to see you." I was told.

I opened the door to my house expecting a huge celebration of some kind. And then, out of the corner of my eye, I saw - mom. I took a short breath. My mind was playing tricks on me. First I see dad at the hospital, and now mom? She was sitting in a chair, bleeding from head to toe. I saw cuts all over her bare feet and she was gagged with her hands bound behind her back.

"Kaylee! What are you --" Kaylee was standing behind my mom with a gun pointed directly at her head. I felt my whole body start to tremble uncontrollably.

"Kaylee!" I repeated. "What are you doing here?? Where have you been?, I thought you were dead" I stopped and drew another breath. I seemed to only have a limited supply of breath available.

"I've been looking all over for you! Your parents and sister are dead, don't you know that?"

Kaylee just stared at me as if in a daze. I waited for her first word.

"Kaylee, say something!" I urged her. I was losing patience fast.

Then the gun went up. It was pointed directly at me.

"Shut up!" were the first words she chose.

"Look, we can talk about this ..."

The gun came closer and closer in my direction.

"Didn't...I...tell...you...to SHUT UP?" Her face was unrecognizable. I missed my old friend Kaylee, and whoever this was standing in front of me - was definitely not Kaylee.

"All these years I had to listen to your bratty ass talk about how *perfect* your family was. So I wanted to show you how *imperfect* your little family actually was." That was not what I expected. Doesn't everyone want a perfect family?

"Kaylee, what are you saying?" I was trying to buy some time, hoping she would lose interest in that gun.

"Hmm, I guess it's time to tell you everything." Everything? What does *everything* mean?

"First, there's your dad." Oh God, she never even spoke much to my dad.

"Do you remember the night I slept over, and I told you I was going downstairs to get some water? I didn't come back until two hours later, do you remember?"

I remembered. I just thought the girl was thirsty. No big deal.

"Well, that's the first night your dad and I made love. I was floating on air because I made love to a *real man* and lost my virginity!"

I felt all my organs shut down and my brain went silent. My cells stopped functioning and I was just a body occupying space. I was able to absorb a lot of bad things before turning 16, but I could never prepare myself for my best friend having an affair with my father.

I continued staring at Kaylee, and not the gun pointed directly at my face.

"Kaylee, are you saying - you had sex with my dad - and you lost your virginity - to my DAD?" Those words just didn't make sense together and I vowed they would never appear in the same sentence ever again.

My best friend laughed like a Disney villain and said "Yes, that's what I'm telling you. Do you want me to repeat it?" Her eyes glowed like a nuclear reactor.

"No", I said. "And I don't believe you." I had to keep her engaged in conversation.

"Oh, believe it, girl. We were madly in love. I would go to his office on those *lunch breaks* where you thought I was hanging out with my *boyfriend*. We would do it all over his office desk!" The image of that disgusted me.

"And remember those nights where he would come home late and tell your mom he had to work?" She continued her villainous monologue. "He was with me at the hotel. My parents didn't know anything, they were so clueless!" Was Kaylee actually capable of a cruelty that rested on a new and sophisticated form of derangement? My breath was rattled. I needed more words.

"So how did you explain being out late?" My mind was searching wildly for questions.

"I told them I had a job. I always had money because your dad made sure of that." The thought of dad giving her money sucked the soul right out of my body. I started to cry.

"SHUT UP!" I'm *sick* of your crying! I wanted to laugh so hard in your face when I came over for your birthday and you asked if you could *confide* in me." She would make the perfect villain for every *Lifetime* movie, I thought.

"How could you be so - so cold to me, Kaylee?"

"Easy" said little Cruella Deville, "I have no heart. *That* was taken from me a long time ago."

I really didn't understand all this - I couldn't comprehend why I was her target.

"But why me?" I blurted out.

"Why NOT you?" said my best friend. "You had everything I ever wanted, but you just flaunted those things in my face. You basically told me I was nothing because I didn't have anything. So I set out to make your life a living hell." The wicked smile forced her gun to come an inch closer to my frozen frame. "It looks like I succeeded. Look at your life now!"

I stared at my mom. I had to help her. She was bleeding so much.

"What did you do to her?" I pointed at mom.

"Your dad told me he would stop seeing me because he loved his wife." Her smile turned to scorn. "He became more and more distant with me. So one night I dressed up in some sexy red-lace lingerie and went to his office. He was working late, of course. He took one look at me and gave in like all men do." I closed my eyes and tried to imagine something other than what she was vividly describing. It's one thing to cheat on mom, but - with her?

"After he was done with me, I stole his credit card while he cleaned up."

Kaylee had committed the perfect crime. Who would ever suspect this innocent child of being so vicious?

"That's when I withdrew $5,000 from his account. I called an escort service and they sent out someone named Jennifer." That name sounded so familiar. "Jennifer was supposed to seduce your dad and take pictures so I could send them to your mom. But then --" Kaylee paused and the gun lowered half an inch. Maybe this is my lucky -- "But then, your dad ended up falling in love with Jennifer and got *the tramp* pregnant!"

Oh my God! My dad fell in love with a prostitute and got her pregnant? Kaylee did all this?

"I found out that your dad proposed to that whore, so I went to her house and told her to confess everything to your mom. If she didn't I was going to kill her and her unborn child."

My mind was slowly putting the pieces of this sordid puzzle together. Jennifer's visit to our house unleashed hurricane Karla onto the Earth. And Kaylee was to blame for all of it!

"So YOU set this whole thing up?" I wanted everyone to hear my victorious puzzle-solving ability.

"Yes, pretty much", said Kaylee, "but some of it played out much better than I expected. Your mom and her killing spree, for instance. Then Karen Ellis and her son Laurence - their untimely demise."

"Wait", I interrupted, "you knew that Laurence was Mrs. Ellis's son?" I had to learn more.

"Sure, how do you think he even ended up at our school?" She expected me to know this already?

"I got him kicked out of boarding school and he had no choice but to come back home and live with his parents. I made sure that both of you and Laurence would meet. Why do you think I was always available when you needed a ride?" How did she have the time to plan all this out? She was too clever for her own good. "I hope you didn't think I enjoyed being your chauffeur!"

She made a terrible chauffeur, and she was now a terrible friend.

I was slowly processing all this in my mind. I was trying to force more words out, but my tongue went on strike. I was better off having an out-of-body experience and was praying for one right about now.

"What's the matter, cat got your tongue?" I had never heard Kaylee say that expression. Only evil people utter that just before they kill someone.

"Wait, did you pay that On Time driver to rape me?"

"Nope, that was just another lucky bonus." A *lucky bonus*? Who would call that a "lucky bonus". This girl was way past deranged. The person I trusted the most - with all of my personal business - betrayed me. She would make Judas proud.

I let a few seconds lapse and then gave her my closing argument.

"So YOU are the cause of my life falling apart?" I waited for a rebuttal.

"Hey, you made it so easy. Your mom also did a great job." She laughed the same way a serial killer laughs. She expertly held the gun in one hand and clapped with the open hand. She even clapped like a serial killer. "I was so happy to see your mom on the run - she made a great fugitive, bravo!"

I wanted Erica to just finish her off now. Where were the cops when you needed them?

"When your mom was on the run, I knew she was out of the picture. I dropped you off at that building, then went back to the hospital, looking sexy for my man." Ugh, please stop saying that! "When I got to your dad's room, I saw your mom leaning over his bed, kissing him. I got so mad when I saw that, so I pulled out my knife." This girl had access to so many weapons! Who taught her to do this?

"I ran up behind your mom and pressed the knife against her back and told her not to move. Then I told your dad that we could finally be together. Do you know what he said to me?"

I didn't know. I didn't want to know. Just get this over with, already.

"He said, I don't want you anymore, Kaylee. I love my wife and family. He gave me the most disgusted look a man could ever give."

Good for you, dad. Even though you did something terrible, you had the courage to end it.

Kaylee continued her rant. "I tied your mom up in the chair. I told your dad that if I couldn't have him, then nobody could. I took an empty syringe and pushed air into his IV tube. He gasped for air until he finally stopped breathing. When the machines started alarming, I grabbed your mom and left. If your mom resisted, she'd be in the Mississippi river by now."

I couldn't believe there was a small chance of getting mom and dad back together again. We could have been the perfect family that we used to be.

"Your mom tried to get away from me, so I hit her over the head with a rock. I put her in the trunk of my car and drove her to my parent's farmhouse in Trenton. That's where I tortured her - look at my work of art over there ..." Kaylee waved the gun in the direction of my mom, bound and gagged in the chair.

"Kaylee". I directed her attention back to me so she wouldn't shoot mom. "I never thought in a million years that you - you would be behind all of this. You're my best --"

"Stop right there. You know what they say - keep your friends close, and your enemies closer, right?" Unbelievable.

"So, what happened to your parents?" I asked.

"Huh, they were in the way, so I had to make it look like an intrusion."

"But what about little Lilly? Your poor little sis --"

"No witnesses. That's the rule, right?" This girl, standing in front of me, truly had no heart. No soul.

I was running out of energy. There was no way of predicting this outcome. I looked around the room and noticed -- "What did you do with KJ? Please tell me --"

"If you're looking for your little brother, he's outside in the back, I mean...in the shed."

My life flashed before my eyes. When I thought Kaylee was dead, I thought my world was over. But now I realized that no one could come between me and KJ. If I lost KJ, I lost everything.

"YOU   KILLED   KJ??"   I   started   to   approach   her, even   though   the   gun   remained   raised   and   pointed. "Not exactly *killed*". She chuckled. I was tired of this serial-killer-wannabe finding fresh humor in destroying lives.

"More like - I chopped his hands off. But if you get to him in time ..."

"GOD you're SICK." Every cell in my body came back to life and wanted to strangle her now.

"Why, thank you, bestie. Or should I just call you *Lexi boo*?"

I only had one wish - to see this girl dead. Just before I did something stupid, the front door opened and Grandma entered the room. Kaylee panicked and the gun went off. A bullet went right through Grandma's head. She was gone. I had to act quickly.

I fell down to the ground and crawled on hands and knees to the kitchen. Then I heard Erica.

"Put your hands up and drop that gun, NOW!" she yelled to Kaylee. *Bang. Bang.*

I prayed for Kaylee's death. That was my last request to God that day. But God had other plans.

"Lexi boo, oh Lexi boo come out, come out wherever you are". I was now the hunted with nowhere to run. This scene was right out of a horror movie. I remained on the floor, shaking visibly. I grabbed Kaylee's leg as she tiptoed past me and she fell hard on the ground. The gun sailed through the air and landed near the closet. We were fighting to reach it but we both remained on the ground. I managed to punch her hard in the face but she somehow grabbed my hair and slammed my face on the floor. People could confuse this for a professional WWE smackdown and I couldn't believe it was happening in my own kitchen.

Kaylee managed to get up and grab the gun. It was now pointed directly over my face.

"Goodbye, *bestie*." Her last words to me were chilling. Then I noticed a shadow behind her.

Bam. Bam. Bam.

Mom was behind Kaylee, striking her with a Louisville Slugger. Over and over and over again. After the final *Bam*, my mom hit the floor. She drew every last breath to finish off Kaylee. I ran over to her and turned her face upward. She was lifeless, with no pulse. She sacrificed herself for me. The phone was in plain sight. I called 911.

"Hello what is your emergency?"

"My best friend just tried to kill me and my mom just killed her --"

"Ok, slow down. Are you okay? Who else is there with you?"

"Hurry, we need a few ambulances"

"Ok, dear, we have units in the area. There on the way."

I remembered what Kaylee said about KJ. I prayed he was still alive. I limped outside to search for KJ and I saw it. One of his hands laying on the ground. *Oh my God, I'm too late!* I instinctively picked up the limb because I wanted to put it in ice - isn't this what they do in the movies? Just then, a body burst through the back door and approached me with the limb still fresh in my hand.

"Freeze, you're under arrest!" It was the police. "Drop the hand and get down on the ground. NOW!"

I couldn't believe it. They were *arresting me? Why?*

"Officer, wait, you have the wrong --"

"Miss, you're under arrest for multiple murders. You have the right to remain silent. Anything you say can and will be used against you in a court of law. You have the right to an attorney. If you can't afford one, then one will be appointed to you by the state..."

"Okay, already. I know my Miranda rights. But you have the wrong person!"

The whole neighborhood heard my screams that day. "I didn't do this. I SWEAR, I didn't do this!" The police ignored my plea. Kaylee won. Her plan was to frame me for all those people who died. I appeared at every crime scene and I was now the main suspect. Kaylee won.

I continued screaming even after they gently placed me in the police car. I knew what police officers did to people who resisted arrest, but there was no way I was going to take this lightly.

With my face pressed against the window, I cried and screamed. Tears were just rolling down the window glass. I cried so hard that my voice became hoarse. I began to slam my head into the window, because at this point everybody I loved and cared about was dead so it was only fair to join them in the after life so that we could become a family again. After two head bangs i suddenly heard...Ring...Ring...Ring. The alarm clock.

I jumped out of my sleep and stared at the rays of sun playfully peeking into my room. There were loud voices coming from the kitchen downstairs. I had to gather my senses. Was this another out-of-body experience? Did I black out from banging my head on the car window? Cold water thrown on my face would be the ultimate judge of that inquiry.

I slowly walked downstairs, expecting to see people tied up, or limbs strewn about the floor. Instead, I was greeted with three very happy people around a table, laughing.

Mom. Dad. KJ. Alive. Laughing. Eating breakfast.

"Good Morning, my beautiful daughter. Sorry, my beautiful, *16 year old* daughter. Happy birthday, baby!"

I walked around the kitchen, touching everything. I caressed mom's face and made sure she was real. Dad was real. KJ was real. Everything around me was real. This was no joke. So what about all the... Oh my Gosh, it was *A nightmare?* On the night before my 16th birthday.

Suddenly the door opened and interrupted my thoughts.

"Lexi! Happy birthday, girl!" Kaylee! It was Kaylee and she didn't have a gun! In place of the gun was a huge box with my name on it. "Happy birthday to the best bestie a girl could ever ask for" she said as she hugged me tightly. The hug cut off my breath but I welcomed it.

"Aw, Kaylee, thank you, girl". It was as if I forgot everything about my dream. Kaylee would never hurt me, at least never in real life. But my face betrayed the events of that horrible dream.

"Girl, what's wrong? Fix that face, it's your Sweet 16! We're going to turn up, ayyy!"

"You're right". She was always right. I smiled at her, wondering about the contents of the box that was handed to me. We all sat down together in the living room, one big happy family. That's the way we started and that's the way we will always end.

My mom sat next to me and started to tear open the box. Whose birthday was this, anyway?

"Hey, Mr. Samuels, you can sit here." Kaylee motioned to my dad as she tapped the spot right next to her. My dad sat down and smiled. He gazed directly into Kaylee's eyes. I looked at both of them for a few minutes. "Hey dad, can you take me to the mall after the party tonight?"

"Oh, what for, " he asked me.

"I have to pick something up that I put on hold at Brandi's Place."

"I'm sorry, sweetpea. I didn't tell you, but ... I have to work late tonight."

"Hey Lex, maybe Kaylee can take you?" Mom was good at coming up with alternatives.

"I already asked her. She said she has to be somewhere tonight before my bday party. It's okay, I can pick it up tomorrow."

"Ok, girl. I'll see you later. I have to drop off something." said Kaylee. She left cautiously, as though she was being watched. She slowly turned around and threw a final glance at my parents. My dad watched her walk out the door. I looked at him then back at Kaylee. My mind started racing and I began to think. "What If my dad and Kaylee were actually having an affair?"

As I kept my gaze on her, a small argument commenced at the bottom of the stairs.

"Why didn't you tell me you had to work tonight, honey? You know it's our baby's special day?"

"It's just work, okay? Don't wait up for me". The argument was over. They both left in a hurry. and I thought to myself "Oh please tell me we are not going back to square one."

Girl, get a hold of yourself. It was only a dream, none of it was real... or was it?

ACKNOWLEDGEMENTS

I'd Like to start off by thanking God for giving me the vision to write this story and to complete it in its entirety. Without him, nothing would be possible. I'd like to acknowledge my mother Paulette Walker who has always supported me and instilled in me that anything is possible in life as long as I don't give up.

I'd like to acknowledge my husband Justin Clarke who poured into me and made sure I finished this book. He kept me accountable and he assisted financially and for all of that, I am thankful.

I'd like to acknowledge Morgan Maccoy Harris with MAM INC who assisted me in lining up the right people to help get this book to where it needed to be and for giving me pointers along the way. I'd also like to give a very special thanks to Mr. Evan Benjamin who went above and beyond the call of duty to make sure that this book would be a hit, with his phenomenal editing skills and timely return. I am forever grateful.

Lastly, I'd like to thank each and every person who supported me by purchasing this book. Without you all, my book would be non existent. Thank You.

9 780578 890548